The Bravest
Princess

e Princess

The Bravest Princess

E. D. BAKER

BLOOMSBURY
NEW YORK   LONDON   NEW DELHI   SYDNEY

Text copyright © 2014 by E. D. Baker
Map copyright © 2014 by Kimberly Bender
All rights reserved. No part of this book may be reproduced or transmitted
in any form or by any means, electronic or mechanical, including photocopying,
recording, or by any information storage and retrieval system, without
permission in writing from the publisher.

First published in the United States of America in April 2014
by Bloomsbury Children's Books
www.bloomsbury.com
Bloomsbury is a registered trademark of Bloomsbury Publishing Plc

For information about permission to reproduce selections from this book,
write to Permissions, Bloomsbury Children's Books,
1385 Broadway, New York, New York 10018
Bloomsbury books may be purchased for business or promotional use. For
information on bulk purchases please contact Macmillan Corporate and
Premium Sales Department at specialmarkets@macmillan.com

Library of Congress Cataloging-in-Publication Data
Baker, E. D.
The bravest princess : a tale of the wide-awake princess / by E. D. Baker.
    pages   cm
Sequel to: Unlocking the spell.
Summary: Sleeping Beauty's younger, nonmagical sister, Annie, still can't rest
while trouble in the kingdom threatens her good friend Snow White.
ISBN 978-1-61963-136-6 (hardcover) • ISBN 978-1-61963-276-9 (e-book)
[1. Fairy tales. 2. Princesses—Fiction. 3. Magic—Fiction.
4. Characters in literature—Fiction.] I. Title.
PZ8.B173Br 2014   [Fic]—dc23   2013034317

Book design by Donna Mark
Typeset by Westchester Book Composition
Printed and bound in the U.S.A. by Thomson-Shore Inc., Dexter, Michigan
2 4 6 8 10 9 7 5 3 1

All papers used by Bloomsbury Publishing, Inc., are natural, recyclable products
made from wood grown in well-managed forests. The manufacturing processes
conform to the environmental regulations of the country of origin.

This book is dedicated to Victoria Wells Arms, my guiding light; Brett Wright, who makes new beginnings joyful; Kim, who makes me laugh and keeps me going; Ellie, who helps me choose; Kevin, my techno-wizard; and my fans, who always want to know what happens next.

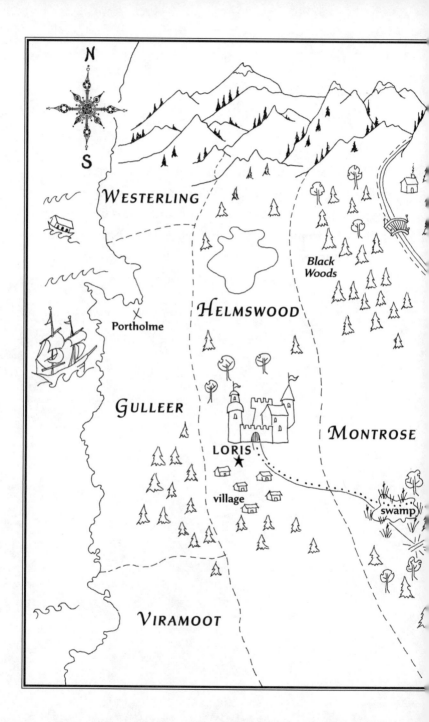

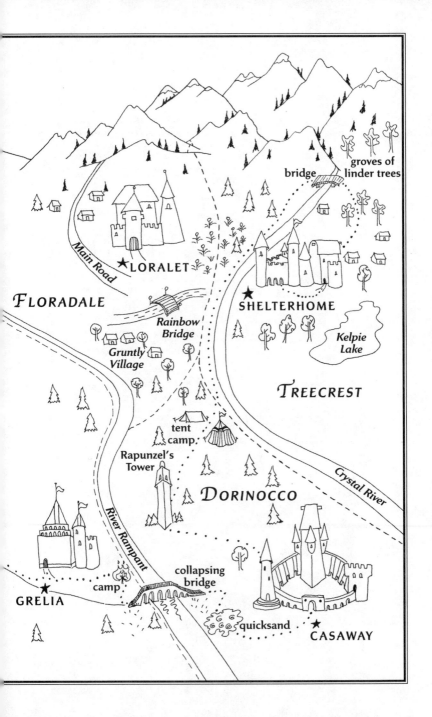

CHAPTER 1

ANNIE STOPPED AT THE TOP of the stairs and smiled when she saw the noisy bustle in the courtyard. While once she might have disliked the commotion, now she thought it was wonderful. For sixteen years her father had refused visitors for fear that one might bring a spinning wheel that could trigger the curse on his oldest daughter. After the curse took hold and everyone else was sleeping, Annie would have given anything to hear the shouting and see the flurry of activity. Now, with the curse ended and her sister about to get married, the entire kingdom had reason to celebrate, and visitors from all over were flocking to the castle.

"Good!" Gwendolyn said as she approached Annie from behind. "You aren't doing anything. Go find Beldegard's sisters for me. A guard told me that he saw the twins out here. I'm having wreaths made for their hair, and I want the woman who's making them to see the girls so she can choose the right flowers."

"First of all, I *am* doing something," said Annie. "I'm looking for Liam because we have an important errand to run. And second, why don't you send a footman to find the twins? I don't even know what they look like."

"They're eight years old with dark hair like Beldegard's. How hard can they be to find? I'm sending you because they'll come if you ask them to, but I've been told that they really don't listen to servants. Please, Annie? Just tell them to come see me," Gwendolyn said, turning on her "I'm so sweet and innocent" look. "I really don't ask that much of you, and this is such a little thing."

"That's not true! You're always asking me to do things for you. Didn't I just get your husband-to-be turned back from a bear to a human? I'll find them, but then I can't do another thing until I run my errand with Liam."

"That's fine," said Gwendolyn. "Just tell the girls to hurry. I want to approve the flowers, and I don't have all day to wait for the twins to show up."

Annie sighed. Her sister seemed to have become friendlier toward Annie while they were searching for the dwarf who had turned Beldegard into a bear, but the old Gwendolyn had returned at the approach of her wedding. Annie hoped that the newer, nicer Gwendolyn would be back after her honeymoon.

Annie was looking for the girls when she spotted Liam walking out of the stable.

His face lit up when he saw her. "Are you ready to go?" he asked. They had commissioned a goldsmith to make a pair of chalices as a wedding gift for Gwendolyn and Beldegard. Annie wanted to pick up the gift herself so it would remain a secret.

"I was, but Gwennie asked me to find Beldegard's sisters. She said that they're out here somewhere. It shouldn't take long to find them if you help me look. They're eight-year-old twins with dark hair like Beldegard's."

Liam nodded. "I think I saw them a few minutes ago. They look a lot like their big brother. If I remember correctly, they were over by the dovecote."

Turning to the far side of the courtyard, Liam led the way through the crowd. When they reached the small, round tower, the girls were nowhere to be seen.

"Hang on," Liam finally said. "Could those two girls be the twins?" He pointed to a pair of girls with long braids making their way through the crowd.

Annie glanced past the dovecote to the open area behind it. "It's possible, but there's nothing back there except a practice field and the dungeon wall. Where do you think they're going?"

"I can't imagine, but they aren't the only ones going that way," said Liam. "Look!" A stream of children of all ages was heading across the open space between the dovecote and the castle wall. When a toddler began to cry, an older girl scooped him up to take him with her.

"They're stopping at that cell window," said Annie. "Are there any prisoners there now?"

Liam frowned. "Your father told me that the only prisoner in the dungeon is Granny Bentbone. Her cousin Mother Hubbard came to see her yesterday."

"I think we should see what's going on. I don't trust Granny Bentbone one bit."

"Then we'd better hurry," said Liam. "Who knows what the old witch will say to the children."

Annie bunched the hem of her skirt in one hand, and together she and Liam dashed across the practice field to where the children were gathered in front of a cell window. As Annie drew closer, she thought she heard the soft hum of magic underlying a familiar voice. Pushing gently through the group of children, she knew why it was familiar. Granny Bentbone, the witch who had lived in a gingerbread cottage and locked children in cages before eating them, was speaking through a little barred opening.

"I'm in here by mistake, dear ones," the old witch was telling the children. "If you let me out, I'll make you some delicious candy!" Annie's father had sent his knights to arrest her and bring her back to the castle only days before.

"She's using magic; I can hear it," Annie murmured

into Liam's ear. "That must have been how she lured children to her cottage in the forest. We have to tell Father. I'm sure he'll want to move her."

"Even the smallest child couldn't get through that window; the bars are too close together. They'd have to go into the dungeon to let her out, and they'll never be able to get past the guards," said Liam.

"I wouldn't count on that." Annie glanced behind them at the children still headed their way. "I'm putting an end to this right now. Excuse me," she said, squeezing past some little boys. When she reached the wall, she remembered that the windows were set so high that neither a prisoner looking up nor a passerby looking down could see much.

"Children, you'll have to move away from here," Annie told them. "You shouldn't talk to this woman."

"She promised us candy!" cried a little girl.

"Then she made a promise that she cannot keep. Don't listen to anything she says. She is not a good person. And as for you, Granny Bentbone," Annie said, turning back to the window, "leave these children alone, and stop trying to talk them into helping you."

"But I don't know why I'm here! I've done nothing wrong!" wailed Granny Bentbone, sounding old and frail.

Annie pursed her lips, not sure what to say. She knew that the elderly woman had difficulty remembering things, although now and then her memory returned for a short time. Either Granny really couldn't remember what she had done, or she was lying to get the children's sympathy. Annie could no longer hear the hum of Granny Bentbone's magic, but from the expressions on the children's faces, the old woman no longer needed it; they already wanted to help her.

"Go on, children," said Liam, shooing them away. "You shouldn't be here."

"Where are Beldegard's sisters?" Annie asked Liam.

"They left when you first told them to," said Liam. "It's just as well. We have to tell your father about this. I'm going to send a guard back here to keep everyone away from the window."

❧

Annie and Liam found the king in his private chamber talking about the progress of the wedding preparations with Queen Karolina and Princess Gwendolyn. The king looked bored and seemed to welcome the interruption. He smiled as they entered the room, but his expression grew grave when Annie said, "We have to do something about Granny Bentbone. We were looking for Beldegard's sisters when we noticed that a group of children had gathered around the witch's cell window. When Liam and I followed them, Granny Bentbone was using magic to draw the children to her and promising them candy if they let her out of the cell."

"I was going to have her executed," said the king,

"but Mother Hubbard demanded that I be lenient in judging Granny Bentbone. If I execute the old witch, Mother Hubbard intends to bring a plague of insects on our linder trees and destroy the crop for the year."

"I can't believe this happened the day before my wedding!" cried Gwendolyn. "I wanted everything to be perfect! I'm going to have only one wedding, and I want it to be the most beautiful wedding anyone has ever seen."

"And it will be," assured the queen. "Halbert, what did you tell Mother Hubbard?"

"Just that I'd find an alternative to execution," said the king. "But I can't keep Granny Bentbone locked away for the rest of her life if she's going to summon children to her anyway. I don't know what I'm going to do now."

"I might have a suggestion," said Liam. "You could send her to that tower where Annie was held prisoner. It's in the middle of a forest, and no one lives anywhere near it. There are no doors, and the only windows are at the top. No one can get in or out of the tower without something to climb, and I doubt the old woman could scale it even if someone gave her a rope."

"That's a marvelous idea!" said Annie. "Granny Bentbone isn't strong enough to climb down anything, and from what I've seen, her magic isn't very strong, either."

"What about Beldegard's sisters?" asked Gwendolyn. "Did you tell them to come see me?"

"I'm afraid the girls left before I could talk to them," said Annie. "They were among the children who had gone to see Granny Bentbone, and we told them all that they couldn't be there."

Gwendolyn stomped her dainty foot and pouted. "I asked you to do one little thing and you failed! Are you trying to ruin my wedding?"

Queen Karolina frowned. "Gwendolyn! Annie was trying to stop Granny Bentbone from harming the children. It's not surprising that she wasn't able to take care of your errand. I'm just glad she noticed what the witch was doing. Thank you for warning us, Annie," she said, turning to her younger daughter.

Gwendolyn sighed in a loud and dramatic way. "Does everything have to be about Annie? Tomorrow is supposed to be my special day!"

Queen Karolina cast her older daughter an annoyed glance. "Annie didn't ask for this to happen."

There was a knock on the door, and a guard poked his head into the room. "A messenger just arrived, Your Highness."

At a gesture from the king, the guard opened the door wide to admit a man carrying a satchel. "I bear two messages from the princess Snow White, Your Majesty," said the messenger. "One is for Princess Gwendolyn, the other for Princess Annabelle."

"I wonder what this is about," Annie said, reaching for her message. Breaking the seal, she spread the parchment open. "Snow White wants me to come visit her the moment I can get away. Her father wants her to choose a prince as soon as possible."

"Read mine, too, Annie," Gwendolyn said, handing her message to her sister. Like most princesses, Gwendolyn had never learned to read. Although she had often made fun of Annie for learning the skill, she usually turned to her sister when she wanted something read to her.

Annie took the message. "Oh, that's too bad," she said. "Snow White and her father are unable to attend the wedding. I wonder what's going on. Something must have happened to keep her from coming here and made her father want her to find a prince right away."

"I can't imagine what it could be," Gwendolyn said. "But I'm sure you'll find out soon enough. In the meantime, could we please concentrate on my wedding? It is tomorrow, you know."

"Yes, we know!" everyone said at once.

CHAPTER 2

"ANNIE, WAKE UP!" Gwendolyn shouted, hopping onto Annie's bed.

Annie opened one bleary eye and peered at her sister. "It's still dark out. Why do *I* have to wake up so early?"

"Because I need to talk to you about Beldegard." Gwendolyn stretched out on Annie's bed and turned to face her sister. "Do you think I've been hasty in agreeing to marry him so soon? I met him only a few weeks ago."

Annie sighed and opened her other eye. "Ordinarily, I'd say that you and Beldegard went way too fast, but you *know* he's the love of your life. He has to be, because it was his kiss that woke you from the curse."

"But I hardly know him! What if he likes things that I don't? What if I don't like his friends or don't get along with his relatives?"

"You'll work it out. I think that finding one's true

love is so rare that you shouldn't let anything get in your way."

"I guess you're right," Gwendolyn admitted. "I really do believe he's perfect for me. I get tingles all over when he kisses me, especially now that he's human! Come on, Annie. Get up! I'm getting married in five hours, and there's still so much to do!"

Annie sat up as her sister hopped off the bed and was surprised when Gwendolyn hugged her. She was sure that if she counted on one hand the number of times any member of her family had given her a hug, she'd still have fingers left over.

"I love you, Annie, and I think you're a wonderful sister. Thanks for our little talk," said Gwendolyn.

Stunned, Annie watched Gwendolyn dance toward the door. As far back as she could remember, this was the first time her sister had ever said she liked her, let alone loved her. All those years before the curse ended, Gwendolyn wouldn't let Annie near her and made cutting remarks about Annie whenever they were in the same room.

"Oh, and one more thing," Gwendolyn said, stopping by the door and turning. "Please don't do anything to disrupt my wedding."

❧

Annie glanced out the window as her bare feet touched the cold stone floor. It was still dark out, and the guards had torches lit by the drawbridge and gates, although when she crossed the room and leaned over the window ledge, she could see the first glimmer of daylight in the east. It looked as if no one else was awake, but she knew that the cooks had been busy for hours preparing the wedding feast, seamstresses had been up all night putting the finishing touches on Gwendolyn's and the queen's gowns, and a small army was already working on the flowers that were to decorate the great hall.

Even as Annie put on her very best gown, she heard the sounds of the castle stirring. Voices rose and fell as people hurried through the hall. A querulous voice outside her door complained about torn stockings. Someone dragged something heavy that bumped and scraped against the floor.

Annie slipped from her chamber, hoping to get something to eat before she got caught up in the bustle of activity around her. When she reached the great hall, she found that most of it had already been decorated with masses of fragrant roses and lilies. She waved at some of the people working in the hall. Growing up with a family who treated her like an outsider, and nobility who had as little contact with her as possible, Annie had spent much of her time with the servants' children and learned a lot from watching the servants work. Her parents weren't happy that she was on such close terms with them, but Annie didn't care.

Annie smiled at Marie, the maid who was in charge of the flowers. Marie knew everything there was to know about flowers and picked fresh blooms every day from the queen's garden. Queen Karolina's fairy godmother had created the garden when Karolina married King Halbert, making sure that the new queen had fresh flowers all year long. As Annie passed by, Marie was telling three footmen where to place several baskets of flowers while she whipped together bouquets using blossoms from water-filled buckets.

Annie looked around as she walked down the aisle between the rows of benches that filled the center of the hall. The tables, which normally stood in two long rows, had been pushed against the wall behind the columns that supported the balcony, where the musicians would be playing. Colorful banners fluttered from the ceiling, garlands of flowers were draped over the balcony railing, and great copper bowls sat on the tables, their blossoms spilling down the sides like froth from overfilled tankards. The scent of the flowers mingled with the fresh beeswax candles in the wall sconces and the sweet-smelling herbs covering the floors, making the entire hall smell like summer.

Two tables had been left at the opposite end of the hall from the dais for the use of anyone wanting breakfast. Annie spotted Prince Emilio, one of the princes she had met while looking for Gwendolyn's true love. Annie joined him, and a moment later, a harried-looking kitchen helper came to the table carrying a pot of porridge. Setting a bowl in front of Annie, the girl began to ladle out a serving. Annie glanced at the porridge, which was laced with burned bits scraped from the bottom of the pot.

"Is there anything else to eat?" she asked the girl.

"I'm sorry, Your Highness," said the girl, dropping another scoop of porridge in the bowl with an audible *plop*, "but that's all there is this morning. The cooks all have their hands full fixing the wedding feast."

"I can't eat that slop," said Prince Digby, who had been Gwendolyn's only suitor before the curse took hold. "It looks like something a cat—"

"Don't you dare finish that sentence," Annie told him. "Some of us are actually going to eat it."

Digby smirked and opened his mouth to continue when a little girl seated at the end of the other table turned to her mother and said, "Momma, I don't feel so good."

"Who was that?" Emilio asked Annie as the woman hustled her daughter from the room.

"I think that was one of the flower girls," said Annie. After pushing the largest blackened bits to one side of her bowl, she tasted the less-burned porridge and decided that it wasn't too terrible. She glanced down the length of the table before asking Emilio, "Where are the rest of the princes?"

"Your Prince Liam is out talking with the guards,

and Beldegard is getting dressed. The others are in their rooms still," said Emilio.

Annie had been hoping to see Beldegard's brother, Maitland, at breakfast. He had told her that he wanted to win Snow White's hand, so he'd probably want to hear about the message she had sent. Annie was wondering if she should send him a message of her own, but then Liam walked in and she forgot all about it. She smiled as he took a seat beside her.

"Your father has decided that the tower is the best place to keep Granny Bentbone for now," said Liam. "He was a little hesitant at first because the tower lies in Dorinocco, but I assured him that it would be all right. My father feels guilty that Mother caused so much trouble when she tried to take over your kingdom, so he's willing to help in whatever way he can. Anyway, your father sent guards ahead to get the tower ready. Tomorrow morning I'm going to accompany the men who are taking Granny Bentbone. I'll go see my father and explain everything after we have the old witch locked away."

Annie glanced up when two girls in matching pale green gowns sat down at the table. Although Annie and Liam had been formally introduced to Beldegard's sisters at supper the night before, the girls acted as if they didn't know anyone. They started a whispered conversation, but within a few minutes their voices rose and Annie couldn't help but hear them.

"I still can't believe how rude those guards were to us," said the girl named Willa. "They should have let us go wherever we wanted. I think we should report them to Father. He would never let guards talk to us that way at home."

Liam leaned forward so he could see past the other people at the table. "Pardon me for interrupting, but where did you want to go?" he asked the girls.

"The North Tower," replied the twin named Tyne, whose braid was already coming undone.

"We weren't doing anything wrong," Willa added, sounding defensive.

Liam sat back and turned to Annie. "The entrance to the dungeon is in the North Tower. Granny Bentbone must still be trying to call the children to her."

"Then she has to leave the castle as soon as possible," Annie replied. "We should tell Beldegard's father about Granny Bentbone. Maybe he can keep his daughters from trying to reach her." She looked up when one of her mother's ladies-in-waiting appeared at the end of the table. "Yes, Lady Clare?"

The middle-aged woman curtsied. "Queen Karolina requires your presence in her chamber."

"I'll be right there," Annie told her. Lady Clare had already begun to walk away when Annie stood and said to Liam, "At least I got a little time to myself."

Liam laughed. "I'm surprised you got away this long."

"So am I," said Annie, straightening her shoulders as if she were heading into battle.

❧

When Annie reached her mother's chamber, she found Gwendolyn in tears and her mother scolding one of the ladies-in-waiting. "Thank goodness you're here, Annabelle!" the queen exclaimed. "I told Lady Cecily to hold on to Gwendolyn's necklace for one minute, but she's somehow managed to lose it. Tell me," she said, turning back to Cecily, "what did you do with the necklace?"

"I don't remember, Your Highness," the girl replied with a nervous tremor to her voice. "I had it in my hand, and then it was gone! Maybe someone used magic to take it!"

"I doubt that," said Annie as she joined them. "Why don't you try retracing your steps?"

When the queen nodded, the lady-in-waiting let her gaze wander around the room. "Well, I was standing over here when you told me to hold it, Your Highness," she said, crossing to a table. "Then I watched Princess Gwendolyn try on the other necklaces. And then you told me to fetch the brush, so I walked past the bed like this and... oh, I know! I set the necklace down here and... look, I found it!" Cecily held up a necklace of sparkling diamonds with a triumphant flourish.

"Good! Try to be more careful next time," said the queen. "I don't know what we would have—"

"Mother!" Gwendolyn cried, a look of horror in her eyes. "Did you see the wreath for my hair? This rose is all wrong!"

"It looks fine to me," said Annie.

"No, no! It's a shade lighter than the others. They all have to be exactly the same!"

"Gwendolyn is right," said the queen. "I don't know how many times I told the woman who arranged the flowers that the wreath has to be perfect!"

"Give it to me," Annie said. "I'll take care of it." Relieved that she had an excuse to leave the room, Annie took the wreath and returned to the great hall. She went straight to Marie and explained the problem.

"Oh dear," said the maid. "I see what she means. I don't know how that got past me. I'll fix it right away."

In just a few minutes, Annie was on her way back upstairs with the wreath. She was only partway down the corridor when she heard raised voices. Peeking into the room, she saw her sister seated on a bench, breathing in short, quick gasps, a look of panic on her face. Her ladies-in-waiting fluttered around her, while Queen Karolina's ladies clustered around the queen, who was telling everyone to stay calm.

"What's wrong now?" Annie asked as she handed the wreath to a lady-in-waiting.

"Marietta and her mother are missing. Marietta is one of my flower girls," Gwendolyn cried.

"Does she have flaxen hair and blue-gray eyes?" said Annie, thinking of the little girl at breakfast.

Gwendolyn nodded. "That sounds about right."

"I'll look for her," said Annie. While the ladies-in-waiting tried to calm Gwendolyn, Annie left the room and hurried down the corridor. Certain that the castle steward would know which rooms were assigned to which guests, she went to the man's office. He wasn't there, so she sent a passing footman to find him.

Nearly twenty minutes passed before the steward appeared, red-faced and apologetic. "I'm so sorry you had to wait, Your Highness!" he gushed, wiping the sweat from his brow with a silk cloth. "I've been running around all morning."

"I understand," Annie reassured him. "I'm looking for Marietta and her mother. Marietta is a flower girl in my sister's wedding. Do you know which room they're in?"

"I do indeed," said the steward. "Marietta is Lady Bentley's daughter. Would you like me to send for them?"

Annie shook her head. "I think the girl might be unwell. I'll go there myself if you'll tell me where to find them."

"I'll have someone escort you," he said, opening the door. He summoned another footman and gave him instructions.

"This way, Your Highness," the footman said, leading the way down the corridor and through the great hall. It took only a few minutes to find the right room. When she learned that the girl had a simple stomachache, Annie sent a maid for ginger tea and told Lady Bentley to get her daughter to the queen's chamber as soon as she was able to. Worried that Gwendolyn might still be panicking, Annie hurried back to her.

"I found your flower girl," Annie told her sister. "She should be here soon."

"Then she'd better hurry. We have to start down to the great hall in just a few minutes," said Gwendolyn. Running her hand across her sleeve, she smiled up at Annie. "Don't you just love the color of my gown? I think it matches my eyes perfectly!"

"Blue for purity!" exclaimed Lady Clare. "That's what all brides wear! Now, Your Highness," she said, approaching Annie with a handful of flowers, "I'm glad you're here. All the princess's attendants are wearing flowers in their hair. Hold still while I put these in. Oh dear, your hair is a tangled mess. Lady Patrice, bring me that brush."

The youngest lady-in-waiting looked sullen when she brought the brush. No one seemed to notice but Annie.

In just minutes, Lady Clare's deft hands had Annie's normally tousled hair brushed until it shone and had fastened flowers among her curls. "You have unusually thick hair. Too bad it isn't a prettier color. Even so, this should do. There, you look very nice," the lady-in-waiting announced. "Come to the mirror and see for yourself."

Guiding Annie to the back of the room, Lady Clare turned her so that she was facing the large gilt-framed mirror on the wall. "That looks better," the woman told her. They both smiled at Annie's reflection. She might not be as beautiful as her sister, or even as beautiful as the ladies-in-waiting, but she did look pretty.

Suddenly Lady Clare gasped. She was looking at her own image and seeing for the first time what she would have looked like if magic hadn't made her beautiful. Her normally shapely nose and lips were thin, and her vivid blue eyes had become pale and set close together. "Oh my!" she exclaimed, her hand flying to her mouth. Casting a horrified glance at Annie, she backed away, saying, "We should probably go now."

Annie was used to this reaction, having seen it for most of her life. Since the day the fairy Moonbeam gave Annie her only magical christening gift, no other magic could touch the little princess. Unfortunately, this fairy-given gift did more than make her impervious to magic. It also reduced the magical gifts of anyone who came near her and removed their magic temporarily if Annie actually touched them. Because all the other members of her family were gifted with beauty, charm, and the talents deemed necessary for royalty, they had learned to keep their distance from Annie. In fact, anyone with any magic had stayed as far from her as possible until the day she broke Gwendolyn's curse and earned the gratitude of everyone in the kingdom.

"I need to talk to Annie," Gwendolyn called from across the room. Gesturing for most of her ladies-in-waiting to stand by the queen, the bride waited impatiently while Annie approached. Gwendolyn spoke in a lowered voice that Annie was sure everyone could still hear. "I've decided that I want you to lead my wedding procession into the great hall. You've done so much for me that I think you deserve the honor."

"That's very nice of you, but I thought Lady Cecily—"

"Lady Cecily is my oldest lady-in-waiting, so she's my maid of honor. She'll walk in right before my flower girls, who will strew petals in my path," Gwendolyn explained.

Annie nodded. "So you want me to walk in first and stand by the wall?"

"Exactly!" said Gwendolyn.

"And as far from the rest of us as possible," Cecily said in a loud whisper.

Annie's fingers curled into fists as she fought not to say what she was thinking, but when she saw the smug look on the faces of the ladies-in-waiting, she couldn't help blurting out, "This doesn't have anything to do with honor. You don't want me near you so you'll stay beautiful." Narrowing her eyes, she studied Gwendolyn's face and saw that her sister's beauty had begun to fade even though they were still yards apart.

"I wouldn't put it like that, exactly," said Gwendolyn.

"Who's going to walk behind Annie?" someone asked.

"Patrice will, of course," said Cecily.

"Why me?" cried Patrice.

"Because you're the youngest lady-in-waiting," Cecily told her.

"It's time to proceed to the great hall, ladies!" announced the queen.

"I'll see you down there," Annie said, her cheeks flaming as she left the room.

Even as she hurried along the corridor, she could hear Patrice cry, "This isn't fair! I want to look beautiful, too!"

"It's not worth getting mad about," Annie muttered to herself. The more she thought about it, the more she was sure she shouldn't have been surprised. A bride would want to look her best on her wedding day, especially when she had the reputation of being the most beautiful princess in all the kingdoms. Even so, Annie couldn't help but feel hurt after all she'd done for Gwendolyn. And she'd thought they were starting to get along so well!

CHAPTER 3

THE CORRIDORS WERE NEARLY DESERTED, so it didn't take Annie long to reach the great hall. The musicians were already playing, though stragglers were still going in. Stepping to the side to let people pass, Annie felt something snag the toe of her shoe. She bent down to look, and someone bumped into her, knocking the flowers from one side of Annie's hair. Before she could pick them up, they were trampled into the herbs on the floor.

The other members of the wedding party had begun to gather in the corridor, forming a line by a different door. Gwendolyn waved to her from the back of the line, then frowned and pointed to Annie's hair.

"Here," Annie said to a passing footman as she handed him the broken flowers. "Please ask Marie for replacements. I need them right away."

The ladies-in-waiting glowered at Annie as she passed them on her way to the front of the line. Lady

Patrice hung back, scowling as if daring Annie to come closer.

Annie waited, nervously looking around for Marie to bring the flowers. Even after the music for the procession started, she dawdled as long as she could. When she finally felt someone tucking flowers into her hair, she would have turned around to thank Marie, but everyone was looking her way. Facing forward with her head held high, she started down the aisle. She was partway to the dais when she glanced back to make sure that Patrice was following her and saw that the lady-in-waiting had let a large gap form between them. Wearing a strained smile, Annie continued walking. When she reached the point where she had to turn, she headed toward the side of the hall, walking far enough from the others that she was standing just past one of the pillars.

Annie couldn't see very much from where she stood other than the flower-covered tables to her left, the pillar beside her, and the backs of some of the attendants. Focused on trying to hear what everyone was saying, she didn't notice the smell at first. When she did, she crinkled her nose and looked around. It was an odd smell, sickly sweet and bitter at the same time. Then the odor changed, smelling as if something was burning.

Fire in a castle was always a danger, with all the fireplaces, torches, candles, and people packed so closely together. The candles near her weren't lit and wouldn't be until later in the day, when the sunlight was no longer streaming through the high windows. It was warm out, so the fireplaces in the great hall weren't lit, either. When she turned her head, the smell seemed to be equally strong in every direction. Suddenly she caught a glimpse of her reflection in one of the highly polished copper bowls on a nearby table. Although her reflection wasn't too clear, she could just make out the shape of her face, the color of the flowers in her hair, and smoke rising from one of the flowers.

"What th—" Annie exclaimed. Bending down, she batted at the flower, knocking it to the ground. It continued to smoke, making the herbs on the floor curl and turn brown around it. Afraid it would start a real fire, Annie yanked the flowers out of the copper bowl and emptied the water onto the smoking blossom. Even when it was lying in a puddle of water, the flower continued to smoke.

Annie turned to see if anyone had noticed, but everyone was singing now and still looking toward the bride and groom. It was up to her to take care of this, and if water wouldn't put it out, she had to find something that would. Using the bowl to scoop up the flower and the herbs turning brown around it, she hurried from the hall down the cleared space between the pillars and the tables.

She was hoping to find something she could use in the kitchen, so she headed down the corridor at a run.

Bursting into the room, she caught the busy cooks' attention by shouting, "I need help!"

"You sure do!" cried one of the kitchen helpers. "Your head is on fire!"

"Quick! Get a bucket of water!" shouted a cook.

"It's not my head, it's the flower in this bowl," Annie said, holding up the bowl to show them.

"Maybe so, but it's your head, too!" yelled a kitchen helper as she dumped a bucket of cold water on Annie.

"Stop!" Annie cried as the scullery maid came running with another bucket. Everyone in the kitchen gathered around her, arguing about what to use if water wouldn't put the fire out.

Annie reached up and was about to touch her head when the cook in charge of the kitchen knocked her hand away. "Don't touch it or you'll burn your hand. Sit down and let me look at this," the cook ordered her, shoving her onto a bench. "There's something in your hair, and it's still burning, even as wet as it is. Get me a knife. I'm going to have to cut this hair out before it spreads to the rest."

"Please hurry!" Annie exclaimed. She could feel the heat of the fire now, which made it all seem more real. The cook hacked away at her hair, dropping the pieces into the copper bowl, where the flower was still burning.

"Careful," said one of the other cooks. "You don't want to touch that green stuff. That's what's burning, isn't it?"

"What's going on here?" Liam bellowed from the doorway.

He turned pale when he saw the cooks gathered around Annie and that one of them was sawing away at her head with a butcher's knife. Taking two steps, he bounded over a broad table and was about to tackle the cook when Annie yelled, "Don't! They're helping me. There was something on a flower someone stuck in my hair. It burned the flower and started burning my hair."

"We're cutting off the hair that's smoking," said the cook, who was still chopping away. "It's odd—there aren't any flames, but it burns as if there were. There, that should do it." Dropping a final chunk of hair into the bowl, she handed the bowl to Liam. "Smells foul, doesn't it?"

"How much did you have to take off?" Annie asked, running her hand over her head.

"More than I wanted to, less than I was afraid I might have to," said the cook. "It's a good thing your hair is so thick or that green stuff might have gotten to your scalp, and you'd have been cooked, so to speak."

"Don't worry, Your Highness. I bet one of those ladies-in-waiting can do something pretty with your hair," said the kitchen helper who had dumped the bucket of water on Annie.

Pursing her lips, Annie tried not to laugh out loud.

They thought she was worried about her hair! It was the person who had tried to kill her that had her worried!

A footman stuck his head into the kitchen. "The ceremony is over and the tables are almost all in place. We can start taking the food out. Oh, I, uh, didn't see you, Your Highness. Is everything all right?"

"It is now," Annie said, although her voice was shaky and it was obvious to her that everything was not all right. Whoever had tried to kill her wasn't using magic. She could defend herself against magic, but not this! "I would like to wash my hair to get the smell out, though," she added, trying to make her voice sound normal.

"I have just the thing," said the head cook. "It's a soap I made myself. I put rosemary and lavender in it, so it smells a lot better than you do right now."

Annie gave her a halfhearted smile.

"You can wash your hair over there," the cook told her, pointing to a corner by the fireplace. "We have too much work to do to heat water for a full bath and have someone haul it upstairs, so you'll have to wash your hair in a bucket. I can spare one of these lazy girls to help you, but be quick about it. I'm going to need her back in a few minutes. Betha, you can help her. I'll get you that soap, then leave me in peace. I have too much to do as it is."

Annie knew Betha would have kept up a constant chatter if Liam hadn't been there. As it was, the girl was in awe of the prince and spent so much time gawking at him that Annie wondered if she ever looked at the hair she was washing.

"Where did you get this flower?" Liam asked, shifting the bowl from side to side as he examined the smoldering remains.

"I already told you," Annie said, leaning over the bucket while Betha rubbed more soap into her hair. "A few of the flowers that Lady Clara had put in my hair fell out when someone bumped into me. I asked to have Marie replace them, but I didn't see who actually put them in. Someone is bound to have seen who did it."

Liam frowned and shifted the bowl again. "I'm going to send this to an alchemist. I want to see if he can identify this green stuff."

"I can tell you one thing," said Annie, flinching when Betha poured cold water over her head to rinse her hair. "That green stuff may smell awful, but it isn't magic. If magic had been involved, it wouldn't have worked so close to me. But that doesn't mean someone didn't use magic to hold it until they had it in my hair so they wouldn't get burned themselves. I didn't hear the sound that magic makes, but then again, the music was loud."

"All done, Your Highness," Betha said. "Now we just have to dry your hair. I'll go see if I can find a bit of clean sacking. Be right back!"

Liam took Annie's hand in his and squeezed it. "Maybe you shouldn't go to the feast. Someone just tried to kill you!"

"I know," said Annie. "And it frightens me more than you can imagine! I've had people try to hurt me using magic many times, but no one has ever used anything like that strange fire. I don't have any way to protect myself from it. I guess that's what scares me the most."

"Don't worry," said Liam. "I'll find out who's behind this. In the meantime, maybe you should stay away from public places."

"I'm not going to hide or change my life because of whoever did this," said Annie. "I just have to be more careful, that's all. Besides, Gwennie would never forgive me if I wasn't there for her feast. It's bad enough that I had to run out during the ceremony."

"Considering the circumstances, I'm sure she'd forgive you," Liam told her, and laughed when he saw her expression. "All right! I can see that your mind is made up. We'll go to the feast, but I'm not letting you out of my sight. Now, whatever you do, don't accept anything from a stranger or let anyone stick anything in your hair, or pocket, or shoe or—"

"Don't worry," said Annie. "I won't! If a stranger comes up to me, I'll shriek and run the other way."

❧

When they entered the great hall, Annie was certain someone would say something about the way she had left the ceremony early, or make a remark about her damp hair, or note the slightly singed smell that still clung to her. Instead, no one said anything as they walked to the front of the room and took their seats at the table with Beldegard's sisters and the visiting princes.

Situated just below the table where the bride, the groom, and their parents were seated, Annie and Liam's table was close enough that they could overhear Gwendolyn when she said to Beldegard, "I think it's so sweet that you wanted Annie to sit near us."

"As I said before, magic or no magic, you will always be the most beautiful princess in all the kingdoms to me," Beldegard told her. "We would never have met without your sister's help, so she deserves to sit up here more than anyone."

"I love that you're a man of honor," said Gwendolyn, squeezing his hand where it rested on the table.

"I really like my gown," Princess Willa announced. Beldegard's twin sisters were wearing pale green gowns with white embroidery on the sleeves and square-cut necklines. Although the gowns had started out look-ing the same, Willa's gown was still clean and neat, without a wrinkle or crease, while Tyne's looked as if she had slept on the ground while wearing it. Annie thought she saw bits of dried herbs from the floor in Tyne's braid.

"It's okay," Tyne said with a shrug. "Wow! Look at the roasted pheasant they just brought in. I want some of that!"

"Everyone looks so beautiful," Willa said, casting an

admiring glance at the people sitting nearby. "Except you," she said to Annie. "I was wondering about that. Why is your sister so beautiful and you're so ordinary?"

"You know why," Tyne said. From the way she shifted in her seat and her sister grunted, Annie thought that Tyne had kicked Willa under the table. "Beldegard told us that magic doesn't work on her. That's why she could help him and why she couldn't get any magical christening gifts. Honestly, sometimes I wonder how we can be twins. You don't remember anything!"

"I remember that you aren't supposed to kick me!" Willa hissed. "I'll get you later!" Suddenly her frown turned into a scowl, and she leaned so close to her sister that they were almost touching. "What's wrong with your face? You don't look like you anymore."

"What are you talking about?" Tyne said, looking annoyed.

Willa giggled. "Your face is changing. Your nose is shorter and you have freckles!"

"Don't laugh at me!" said Tyne. "I can see freckles popping out all over your face!" She gasped and turned to Annie. "It's because of you, isn't it? It's that whole thing about magic not working around you! Willa, this is what we'd look like if magic didn't make us beautiful!"

Willa gasped. "I bet you're right! Look at Maitland! He looks different, too! Everybody does, except for you, of course," she said to Annie. She turned to look at Liam. "And you. Why is that?"

"Because he must not be handsome because of magic," said Tyne. "He's handsome even without it!"

The princes all knew what happened when they were near Annie, having been near her before, but none of them seemed to care much.

"Tell me, how was your trip here?" Emilio asked Willa.

Annie gave him a grateful glance when the twins began to chatter about everything they had seen on the way there. When she heard a sound at the next table, she glanced at her own sister. Gwendolyn was nibbling on a quail egg while a serving maid offered a platter of beef to Beldegard. Annie noticed that the prince had helped himself to the best-looking slice and placed it on Gwendolyn's plate.

"Oh, Beldegard," breathed Gwendolyn. "You are so chivalrous!"

"I can't stand to look at them," grumbled Prince Digby. "The way they gaze into each other's eyes makes me ill."

"I must say, I'm happy for Beldegard," said Maitland. "I think he and Gwendolyn suit one another very well."

"Not as well as Eleanor and I suit each other," said Annie's and Gwendolyn's cousin, Prince Ainsley. "I knew we were meant to be together the moment I saw her." He turned to look at the girl seated beside him, placing his hand over hers.

"With a little help from her fairy godmother," Annie

murmured to Liam. "He would never even have met Cinderella if it hadn't been for the fairy Moonbeam."

"I can't believe Gwendolyn and Beldegard are actually married," said Prince Andreas, whom Annie had met on her quest for Gwendolyn's true love. "I came all this way hoping that he'd turn back into a bear, or she would decide that she didn't like him after all. And for what? They're married and I'm still without a bride. My parents are going to make my life miserable when I go back home. They let me come only because I was sure I still had a chance with Gwendolyn!"

"Cheer up!" Gwendolyn exclaimed, beaming at the princes. "I have good news to share with you. A friend of mine, Princess Snow White of the kingdom of Helmswood, is looking for a prince to marry. Not only is she very beautiful, she is the only child of the king. The prince who marries her will rule at her side one day."

"Really?" murmured Cozwald. He was Emilio's cousin and another prince who had wanted to marry Gwendolyn. "I've heard that Helmswood is a very wealthy kingdom."

"Didn't they have some sort of problem with a nasty witch recently?" asked Emilio.

"Who hasn't?" said Digby. "I think I should pay Helmswood a visit and let the princess see what a real prince is like."

"I believe I'll go there as well," said Andreas. "My

parents will understand as long as I come back married to somebody."

"If you're all going, I suppose I should go, too," said Emilio. "I may never get another chance like this."

Maitland looked stricken when he heard the other princes announce their intentions. Annie couldn't help but feel sorry for him when she saw his expression. "Poor Maitland," Annie whispered to Liam. "He's going to have competition for Snow White's hand. You know, if they all converge on Snow White at once, that sweet girl won't know what to do. She asked me to go see her, but I think she's going to need my help more than ever now. You said you were leaving in the morning to help take Granny Bentbone to the tower?"

"As soon as the sun comes up," said Liam.

"Then I'm going with you," Annie announced. "We'll drop off Granny, visit your father, and go to Helmswood as quickly as we can. Snow White won't know what to do when all these princes show up, and I want to be there to help her. Besides, she liked Maitland until she overheard him talking to his friends about her father's throne. The more I've gotten to know him, the more I think he actually is a good person, and I'm afraid she won't give him a chance. I'd like to talk to her before she makes any decisions."

"But it will be her choice," said Liam.

"Of course!" said Annie. "I just want to be there to make sure she makes the right one."

Chapter 4

"I suppose I should ride in the carriage with Granny Bentbone," Annie said with a sigh, tugging her cloak high around her neck to ward off the chilly morning air before pulling on her gloves. She stepped back as four of the guards accompanying them rode to the front of the line, preparing to get under way.

Liam glanced up from checking his horse's girth. "I thought you were going to ride with me."

"I *want* to ride with you, but I don't trust the old woman. We don't know how she lures children to her, or what other magic she can do. We'll be passing through some villages and I'm afraid she'll use her magic on more children. I think someone should ride in the carriage to keep an eye on her. I'm the only one her magic can't affect, so I should be the one to go with her."

"I was looking forward to talking to you," Liam said,

giving his horse's girth an extra hard tug. The stallion grunted and stepped to the side, flicking his ears back as he glanced at Liam.

"You could ride in the carriage, too," said Annie. "I know you don't like Granny Bentbone any more than I do, but at least we could be together."

"But we couldn't talk in front of her. I know! Let's put a gag in her mouth and truss her up like a goose. That should stop her from using her magic, and neither of us would have to ride in the carriage," said Liam.

Annie shook her head. "I don't want to be cruel, even to someone as horrible as Granny Bentbone."

Liam opened his mouth to say something, but when he saw the look on Annie's face, he shook his head and said, "No, you're right. I'll go with you. I don't want you riding alone with her. We'll tie our horses behind the carriage so we can ride them once we're past the villages."

While Liam talked to Horace, the elderly guard, Annie climbed in. Granny Bentbone was on the front bench facing backward, so Annie took the seat facing forward, across from the old woman. A chain clanked when the witch shifted her feet; the guards had chained her wrists and ankles together so she couldn't jump out.

"What do you want?" the old woman snapped. "If I'd wanted company, I would have said so."

"I'm here to make sure you don't try to work your magic on anyone," said Annie.

"Magic? What magic?" the old woman said, but from the sly look on her face, Annie was sure the witch was lying.

"Behave yourself, and you can sit there in comfort. Try to use your magic, and you'll be tied and gagged."

"You don't know who you're talking to!" Granny Bentbone snarled.

"Apparently, neither do you," said Annie.

The old witch cackled and leaned toward Annie. "If you know about my magic, you should be afraid of me."

"If you knew me better, you'd know why I'm not afraid," Annie replied.

It was true that she wasn't afraid of the old witch. Fairies and witches had tried to use their magic on Annie, but it always bounced back onto them. Annie had been impervious to magic her whole life and had grown up unafraid of it. Being attacked in a way that didn't involve magic was much more frightening to her. Annie was as vulnerable to that kind of danger as anyone else.

Both Annie and Granny Bentbone turned to the door as it swung open, and Liam climbed into the carriage. Annie moved over so Liam could sit beside her.

"How many more people do you plan to stuff in here?" grumbled Granny Bentbone. "I need room to stretch my legs or they'll cramp."

"This is going to be a very long day," Liam murmured.

The carriage started with a jolt, making Granny

Bentbone lurch so that she almost fell to the floor. Muttering to herself, she wiggled back onto the seat and wedged her body into the corner. "I hate carriages!" she announced.

"You're not the only one," said Liam.

Annie glanced out the window beside her. Metal bars had been added to the windows the night before. Black fabric had also been draped on either side to cover them if necessary, but Annie left the window uncovered so she could look out. Because most of the castle's inhabitants were just beginning to stir, there was hardly anyone around to see the travelers leave. Annie could hear the riders in the front clatter over the drawbridge and braced herself as the carriage rattled across the uneven boards. They were just getting started, and she already couldn't wait for the trip to be over.

They took the road headed north, passing through the village of Shelterhome soon after leaving the castle. It was still early enough that there were few people on the streets, and only a couple of them were children. Granny Bentbone leaned toward the window, peering out, but the carriage was traveling so quickly that the children were left behind before Granny could try to do anything.

After passing through Shelterhome, Granny Bentbone closed her eyes and seemed to fall asleep. Liam let his eyes drift closed as well. As the carriage bumped down the uneven road, Annie wondered how anyone could possibly sleep. All the roads in Treecrest had deteriorated after years of neglect. When her father had banished spinning wheels from the kingdom to keep Gwendolyn from touching one, he had taken away one of the main sources of income for the kingdom. As soon as the curse was over, he immediately began to import spinning wheels into Treecrest, and the kingdom had once again begun to prosper. Annie had heard her father talk about repairing the roads, but so far only those closest to the castle had been fixed.

While Liam's breathing slowed as he fell into a deeper sleep and Granny Bentbone snored, Annie stared out the window at the vast groves of linder trees that covered the countryside. After miles of looking at the same trees, her mind wandered. She was startled when Granny Bentbone woke up with a snort and looked around. "Why am I in a carriage? Where are we going?" the witch asked, her voice becoming shrill.

Liam awoke, looking annoyed. Annie took a moment to study Granny Bentbone. The old woman no longer had the sly look she'd worn earlier, and she seemed to be genuinely confused and frightened.

"You're going to a peaceful place where no one will bother you," said Annie.

"Is it in the forest?" asked Granny Bentbone. "I do so like the forest."

"Yes, it is," said Annie.

"Good," the woman replied, then peered more closely at Annie. "Do I know you?"

"We've met a few times," Annie replied.

"Ah," said Granny Bentbone. "What happened to your hair? It looks like a rabid squirrel made a nest in it."

When Annie's hand flew to the top of her head, Liam snorted. Annie glared at him, and his snort turned into a cough.

After the wedding feast, she had asked Lady Clare to do something with her hair to hide the damage that the fire and the cook's knife had done. The lady-in-waiting had evened it out, then suggested that Annie wear it piled on top of her head. That worked, but Annie hadn't seen the need to wear it up when she was going to spend the day in a carriage with a witch.

"Someone cut it," Annie said.

"Well, they didn't do a very good job," Granny Bentbone said, yawning. A moment later she closed her eyes again and nodded off to sleep.

Annie turned to talk to Liam, but he was asleep as well.

It was midmorning when they approached the bridge that crossed the Crystal River. The noise of the horses' hooves and carriage wheels on the wooden boards nearly drowned out the sound of the rushing water, but when they reached the dirt road on the other side, Annie could hear children playing at the water's edge.

Annie spotted them tossing stones into the water, watching them until she heard Liam say, "What are you doing, old woman?"

When Annie turned from the window, Granny Bentbone was gesturing with her bound hands and muttering under her breath. Certain that the witch was trying to use her magic to call the children, Annie yanked off one of her gloves and threw it at her while shouting, "Stop that!"

Granny Bentbone spluttered and threw up her hand too slowly to block the glove, which hit her cheek and fell to the floor. "How dare you!" screamed the old woman. With a flick of her wrist, she sent a ball of buzzing black lights at Annie. The lights hit Annie, but rebounded onto Granny Bentbone, making her gasp and fall back against her seat, her hands falling rigid onto her lap.

"What have you done?" she cried, struggling to lift her hands, which seemed to be frozen in place.

"I didn't do anything," said Annie. "You did that to yourself!"

"I should have eaten you when I had the chance!" Granny Bentbone shouted at her.

"And I should have knocked your entire cottage on your head!" Annie replied. She had escaped from Granny Bentbone's gingerbread cottage by dissolving a candy support pillar. It was the same day she had rescued two children the witch was going to eat. And now this horrible woman wanted to use children to help her escape her punishment! Annie resolved not to take her eyes off the woman again. However, when she saw Granny Bentbone's arms shaking as she tried to move her frozen hands, she realized that she might not have to.

"You need to use your hands to do your magic!" Annie cried.

"Don't look so happy," Granny Bentbone barked. "This spell will wear off, and when it does, I'll teach you a lesson you won't forget!"

"I wouldn't threaten anyone if I were you," Liam said, his hand going to his sword.

"You mean your spells aren't permanent?" asked Annie.

"Not lately," the old witch said grudgingly. "Nothing works the way it used to. I wasn't even sure I could still do magic like that." Her expression turned bitter, and she scowled at Annie and Liam. "You two think you're so clever, don't you? Well, I bet you haven't even noticed the crows." Her eyes flicked to the window across from her.

"What crows?" Annie asked. She turned to look behind her and cried "Oh!" in surprise.

Two large crows were perched on the window frame, peering between the bars. When the crows saw Annie looking at them, one snapped his beak at her, and they both flew off, cawing.

"I've never seen such brash crows before," said Annie.

"Humph!" said Granny Bentbone. "Those weren't ordinary crows. They're in thrall to a witch, doing her bidding wherever they go. You could tell by their eyes. You would have seen it if you were half as smart as you think you are!"

Liam frowned at the woman. "They aren't your crows, are they?"

"Hah!" Granny Bentbone laughed. "If I were strong enough to control birds like that, do you really think I'd be sitting here talking to you? Controlling children is one thing, but controlling animals takes a truly powerful witch. There aren't very many who are that strong around here."

"Do you know any?"

"A few, and each one is a nasty piece of work. No one comes away from dealing with them unscathed. Why, when I was young, I was a vegetarian! Then I met Horrible Griselda. She enslaved me for a year, and look at me now! You don't think I eat children because I want to, do you? It was forced on me! I'm a victim here! Why, I'd rather eat a nice carrot or—"

"You might as well stop now. I don't believe you," said Annie.

Granny Bentbone shrugged. "It was true. All except for the part about the carrot."

The carriage slowed as they turned south onto a

road that cut through the countryside all the way to Loralet, the capital of Floradale, and south into Dorinocco. It was a well-traveled road and in good condition. Annie hoped that would mean they'd move more quickly now.

Only a few minutes later, Captain Sterling, the captain of the guard, rode back to talk to them. "I've traveled this road many times," he said through the window as his horse kept pace beside the carriage. "There's a stream with very pure water up ahead. I suggest that we stop to water the horses. You can get out to stretch your legs if you'd like, and we can have something to eat. The cooks sent a basket filled with food."

"It's about time," grumbled Granny Bentbone. "I'm so hungry I could eat a horse."

"Sorry," said the captain. "We don't have any horses to spare."

At least she doesn't want something worse, Annie thought, remembering the cookbook she'd found in Granny's cottage. "She told me a few minutes ago that she'd really like a carrot."

"Then you're in luck!" Captain Sterling told the old woman. "I think we might be able to find one in the basket."

When Granny looked confused, it occurred to Annie that she didn't remember what she'd said.

Annie was happy to get out of the carriage when they arrived at the stream. While Liam went to check on their horses, Annie listened to Granny Bentbone complain that she was stiff and needed to stretch her legs, too. Horace helped the old woman out, and four other guards walked her across the road and back. Liam came to escort Annie to the stream, and they went down to the edge together. Fresh and clean, the water was the purest Annie had ever tasted. After drinking her fill, she splashed some on her face, then sat back to watch Liam scoop water onto his face and the back of his neck.

He shook his head, sending droplets flying. "I needed that," he said, wiping trickling water from his forehead. "Maybe I'll be able to stay awake now."

"Why are you so tired?" asked Annie. "I thought we could talk when Granny Bentbone fell asleep, but you slept as much as she did."

"I was up half the night looking for the person who tried to kill you," he said. Running his fingers through his hair, he smoothed it back from his face. "I must have talked to half the people in the castle, but nobody could tell me a thing."

"Why didn't you tell me?" asked Annie. "I could have helped you."

"And what if I'd found the one who did it?" Liam replied. "I wasn't about to bring you two together so your would-be killer could have another chance."

"So now you're keeping things from me?"

"Only what you're better off not knowing," said Liam.

A shadow flashed across the water, and they both looked up. Two crows were there, circling overhead. They settled in the branches of a neighboring tree, their eyes never leaving Annie. "I think I'll eat in the carriage," she told Liam. "I'd like to get on our way as soon as we can."

"Fine with me," he said, turning to look up at the crows. "Does your desire to leave so soon have anything to do with those birds?"

Annie shrugged. "I just don't like the way they're looking at me."

"I was going to ask if you wanted to ride horseback now. There aren't any more villages between here and the tower, so we won't have to worry about Granny's magic luring children. However, if you're concerned about those crows, I suppose you'd rather ride in the carriage."

"I would, at least for now. You don't mind, do you?"

"No," said Liam. "It's fine as long as you don't try to talk me into riding in the carriage with you. I can't sit in that little box with that old witch for another minute. It felt like I was suffocating in there. Too bad we didn't bring another carriage so you wouldn't have to share one with Granny Bentbone. Maybe the fresh air will help me think, and I'll be able to come up with a way to get rid of those scary old crows for you."

"I didn't mean—" Annie began, but she wasn't sure what she'd meant, so she let Liam walk away as she climbed back into the carriage with some bread and cheese and an apple. She wasn't *afraid* of the crows—or was she? They did make her nervous, and Granny Bentbone's talk of evil witches had set her on edge, but was she really afraid of a couple of birds? Liam didn't seem to think she needed to worry about them. In fact, he'd acted as if she was silly to let them scare her. If she was scared, that is.

A few minutes later, two of the guards brought Granny Bentbone back to the carriage while the rest led the horses to the stream to drink. Annie noticed that the witch's spell had already worn off and the old woman was once again able to use her hands. She was still befuddled, however, and looked around the carriage as if she'd never seen it before. The look she gave Annie also seemed to be one she'd give a stranger, but she took the food the guards offered her without question and began to eat as if she really was starving.

It wasn't long before they were on their way again. Annie nibbled her food as she watched the scenery pass by, but Granny Bentbone gobbled hers, eating every last crumb and licking her fingers afterward. Wiping her hands on her gown, she turned and peered at Annie.

"What happened to your hair?" she asked. "It looks like a rabid squirrel made its nest in it."

"Nothing," snapped Annie, not wanting to have the same conversation all over again.

Granny Bentbone shrugged and turned to the

window. When Annie finished eating, she shoved her apple core between the bars of the window beside her. She thought she heard a crow caw, and jerked her hand back when a shadow blocked the sunlight. The old woman laughed, and Annie could feel her face turn red. Maybe she was afraid of the crows a little.

As the miles rolled by, Annie struggled to stay awake so she could keep an eye on the witch. Granny Bentbone dozed, waking up now and then to look around, switch positions, and fall back to sleep again. The sun was low in the sky when they finally stopped for the night at the edge of a forest. Horace opened the door to let Annie out, and Liam was waiting to help her step down.

"If we kept going, we'd be spending the night in the Dark Forest, and that's something I'd rather avoid," said Liam. "We'll set up camp here and reach the tower by midday tomorrow."

"We've slept under the stars before, but what are we going to do about Granny Bentbone?"

"Make sure she's well chained and lock the carriage door," said Liam. "There aren't any homes around, so she won't be able to call any children to her."

Annie glanced back at the carriage. "She has other kinds of magic, but she needs to use her hands to do it."

"That's good to know," Liam told her. "We'll tie her hands together so she can't use them."

"Is anyone going to feed me?" Granny Bentbone

called from inside the carriage. "I haven't had a thing to eat all day, and I'm starving."

Liam raised one eyebrow. "I thought she ate when we did."

"She did. She was very coherent this morning but has gotten forgetful again."

"I'm not forgetful!" cried Granny Bentbone. "My mind is sharp as a . . . a . . ."

"I see," said Liam. "I was just going to say that I know it's early, but if we go to bed soon, we can get a good night's sleep and an early start in the morning."

Annie glanced at the crows, which had already settled on an overhead branch. "I don't know how well I'm going to be able to sleep, but I'm willing to give it a try."

After a simple supper of cold meat and fruit from the basket, Captain Sterling had the guards erect tents, tie and chain Granny Bentbone, and lock her in the carriage before setting up a watch rotation. The last time Annie and Liam had traveled together, they hadn't had guards, horses, or tents, so having any one of these felt like a real luxury. Annie thought about this as she lay in her tent, wondering why, even though she was so much more comfortable, she wasn't enjoying their trip. Of course, part of it was because she was riding in a carriage with Granny Bentbone, who didn't have anything nice to say. Mostly, Annie thought it was because she wasn't alone with Liam. Even when Gwendolyn and

Beldegard had been with them, Annie and Liam had often walked by themselves. Annie enjoyed the times they were alone together more than any other—although she did not like that he was keeping things from her.

Tired from the ride, Annie soon drifted off, but it wasn't long before a sound woke her. She lay there without moving, listening, but when she didn't hear anything else, she decided that she was imagining things and once more fell asleep. A short time later, something woke her again, and this time she couldn't go back to sleep. She was still awake when she heard something hit the tent. For the rest of the night, she dozed off and on, woken many times by small thuds.

The first songbirds were starting to greet the day when Annie crawled out of her tent, yawning. One glance told her what had kept her from a sound sleep. Acorns littered the ground around her tent, even though the nearest oak tree was at least two hundred feet away and there weren't any acorns around the other tents.

"Ouch!" she cried when something hit her shoulder. She looked up to see a crow flying overhead. An acorn rolled to a stop beside her.

"What's wrong?" asked Liam, sticking his head out of his tent.

"The crows have been pelting my tent with acorns. And that one just hit me with one." Annie pointed at the crow, which cawed and landed in the tree. "I'm glad we had the tents to sleep in. I think these crows are trying to torment me."

The crow cocked its head to the side as if considering what she'd said.

"They're just birds, Annie," said Liam.

Annie shook her head. "I think they're more than that. They're too smart, for one thing. They followed us all the way here and won't stop looking at me. Granny Bentbone said that they're in thrall to an evil witch, but I don't know why a witch would do this."

"You don't mean to say that you think those are the same crows that we saw by the stream yesterday?" said Liam.

"I don't know. Crows all look the same to me, but I suppose it's possible. Granny Bentbone said she can see something in their eyes. They seem normal, as far as I can tell."

"Evil witch, huh?" Liam said. "We have run into a few."

Annie shuddered. "I'd rather not talk about it out here, where they can hear us."

"You're joking, right?"

"No, I'm not," Annie declared. "And I'm not being silly, either!"

CHAPTER 5

IT WAS MIDAFTERNOON when they reached the tower where Annie had been kept prisoner. She had climbed down from the tower after braiding the long hair that the previous prisoner had left behind. Now, looking up at the windows from the ground, she wondered how she had ever managed it. The structure was as tall as a castle turret and stood by itself in the middle of a vast forest. Annie was certain that if Liam hadn't been with her, she would never have found it again.

The four guards King Halbert had sent ahead to ready the tower for Granny Bentbone reported to Captain Sterling while Annie and Liam studied the windows high above. A few minutes later, the captain approached Liam.

"The men have a basket rigged up on the other side, Your Highness," he said. "They plan to use it to haul the witch to the top."

"Did they restock the tower and clean up all the hair?" asked Annie.

The captain smiled. "They did indeed. It took two men most of a day to get all the hair out."

"I'd like to see what they've done," Liam said, turning to Annie. "Would you like to go with me? We can see how the basket works."

"It will carry only one person at a time, Your Highness," said the guard. "But it is perfectly safe. The men have been using it to carry up supplies."

Annie, Liam, Captain Sterling, and Horace rounded the tower, leaving most of the guards behind with the carriage and Granny Bentbone. Although Annie knew there had been a lot of long blond hair draped over everything inside, she was surprised to see the size of the pile of hair at the building's base. Waist high and as wide as a large man was tall, the pile looked almost like spun gold. On top of the pile was the rope she'd made by braiding some of the hair, coiled in a giant loop.

"We should probably burn that," said Liam. "We don't want anyone else using it to climb up or down."

"I'll see to that," said Horace, eyeing the pile of hair.

"The basket doesn't look very big," Annie said, examining a large wicker box tied to a rope that ran up and over a pulley fastened to the wall above the window.

"It's big enough for the old witch," said the captain.

"I'll go up first, just to make sure you'll be all right in it," Liam told Annie.

Captain Sterling summoned two of his men to help while Liam climbed into the basket. It was too small for him to sit down, and the sides came up only as far as his hips. He had to hold on to the rope to keep his balance, and the basket started swaying the moment it left the ground.

Annie grew nervous as she watched from below, no longer certain that she wanted to go up the tower. But then Liam was at the window and the basket was on its way back down.

"I'm not so sure about this!" Annie shouted to Liam.

"It really isn't bad," he called down. "Just climb in and close your eyes. We'll pull you up and tell you when to get out."

Annie took a deep breath as the basket hit the ground. Horace helped her over the side, and she grabbed hold of the rope before the basket started moving. When she was a few feet off the ground, Annie closed her eyes, but the basket swayed and bumped into the wall when she wasn't expecting it, jarring her so that her teeth clacked together. She was so frightened that she couldn't have spoken if she'd wanted to, but she opened her eyes and kept them open so that she was prepared for the next bump and could brace herself.

The acrid stench of burning hair billowed in a cloud of smoke around her. Apparently Horace had started the fire. A few more tugs on the rope and she was higher than the smoke and was breathing fresh air again.

Finally, she reached the window, and Liam was waiting there to help her over the ledge. Pulling her into the room, he held her in his arms until she stopped shaking.

"I don't know any other princess who would do what you just did," he whispered into her ear. "You're the bravest girl I know."

"I was terrified," she told him.

"And yet you did it, which shows just how brave you are. No one is being brave when they do things that don't frighten them."

"Maybe," said Annie. "But I really don't look forward to getting in that basket again. Let's do what we came to do and get out of here." Annie turned to look around the circular room. "I'd forgotten just how much I hate this place."

Hand in hand, they walked around the tower room while Annie told Liam what it had been like when she had been there. "Everything was covered with long blond hair, and when I say long, I mean yards and yards. Well, you saw the pile of hair down below. Just imagine it strewn all over everything. The girl who used to live here left dirty clothes and stale food everywhere, too. The bedclothes were so disgusting that I had to sleep on the floor right over here. And I tied the braid to this table before climbing out the window. I must admit, Father's men did a good job getting this place ready for Granny Bentbone. It looks as if they cleaned everything. They put fresh bedding on the bed and even got the bird droppings off the floor under these rafters."

"I understand they completely restocked the larder," said Liam. "She'll live in greater comfort than she would have in the dungeon."

"No one will hear her," Annie said, glancing out the closest window. "And she won't be able to get down on her own."

"What about her magic?" asked Liam. "Didn't you say she could do something other than call children to her?"

"Yes, but she told me that it isn't very reliable. I doubt that she'd be able to use it to escape."

Liam nodded as he surveyed the room. "I think this will do very well. I know I suggested it, but I wasn't sure it would really work until now."

"If you've seen enough, can we go? I'd like to get down from the tower and feel the solid ground beneath my feet again."

"You go first this time," said Liam. "I'll wait until the men bring up Granny Bentbone so I can help them take the pulley down."

Annie bit her lip as she glanced out the window to the ground below. *I can do this*, she thought. *I climbed down on a rope made of hair last time. The basket has to be better than that.*

She tried to look brave as Liam helped her climb into the basket, and he kissed her before letting her go. Gripping the rope so hard with both hands that her knuckles were white, she faced the stone wall and tried not to think about how far she was from the ground. Annie groaned softly each time the basket dropped lower.

She was nearly a third of the way down when something hit the basket from the side, making her lose her balance. Staggering, she clung to the rope and fought to stay on her feet. At first she thought that the basket had bumped something on the wall, but then Liam cried out and she looked back to see a crow swooping toward her.

"Go away!" she screamed when she saw that the crow was flying straight at the basket. It flew so close that she felt the brush of its wings on her arm as she tried to fend it off. She wasn't quick enough, however, and the crow hit the basket, making it twirl on the end of the rope. That little bit of contact had one effect, however; Annie's touch had removed whatever magic had been controlling the crow and it flew off, squawking.

"Get away from her!" Liam shouted from above as the other crow circled closer. "Hold on, Annie. We'll let you down faster."

"I think I'm going to be sick," she groaned as the basket continued to turn.

Horace shouted, and Annie looked down. The first crow had returned, and both birds were flying toward her now, cawing so loudly that they sounded more like some ancient beast than a pair of crows.

There was a rumble below as the carriage rounded the tower. One of the birds landed on the basket's rim and tried to peck Annie. She beat at it with one hand while holding on to the rope with the other, but the crow's weight and movement tipped the basket to a perilous angle, nearly dumping Annie out, and the bird fell off, squawking. Annie clung to the rope with both hands, trying to use her own weight to right the basket as it twirled and banged against the tower, but the second crow had flown higher than the first, pecking at the rope. The rope jerked and shuddered so badly that Annie was certain the whole thing was about to fall.

"Hold on, Annie!" Liam shouted.

The basket dropped four feet with a sickening lurch as the men hurried to lower her. Annie glanced over her shoulder and saw the crows coming toward her again.

An arrow whistled past her, hitting one of the crows. It tumbled over and over as it fell to the ground. The other bird screeched and flew off.

The basket dropped again, and again, and it wasn't long before it settled on the ground. Captain Sterling helped Annie out, but she was holding on to the rope so tightly that he had to pry her fingers loose. He supported her as she staggered a few steps away from the tower. When she couldn't walk any farther, she said, "I need to sit down," and then her legs collapsed beneath her. When she realized that the captain was hovering over her, she patted his hand and gave him a weak smile. "I'll be fine. Go do what you need to do so we can leave this place as quickly as possible."

Captain Sterling hurried off, shouting at his men to bring the witch. Annie turned to the tower and saw Liam climbing down the rope hand over hand, pausing now and then to cast anxious glances in her direction. She looked up when someone stopped beside her.

"That guard shouldn't have shot that crow," said Granny Bentbone. "Now she'll be furious."

"Who?" asked Annie.

"The witch who sent the crows, of course. Just because magic can't touch you doesn't mean that she can't harm you. Her crows are proof of that. There's always a way around obstacles—even a spell that defies magic." Granny Bentbone craned her neck to gaze at the top of the tower. "It's too bad the crows weren't more effective. Ah, well. I'm sure she'll have better luck next time."

"That's an awful thing to say!"

"Why? I was fine until you showed up at my cottage. And every time I think you're gone, you show up like a bad penny. I'd be thankful to any witch who got rid of an interfering busybody like you, and this is just the witch to do it. You may not be afraid of me, but you should be very afraid of her."

"Come along, witch," said Horace. "It's time you saw your new home."

"At least I'll have a room with a view," Granny Bentbone said with a chuckle as the guard led her away.

When Annie glanced at the tower again, she saw that Liam had already reached the ground and was headed toward her. "Are you all right, my love?" he asked, scooping her into his arms.

"I'm fine," said Annie. "Although I don't think you'll ever get me in a basket again."

"I hope you never need to," Liam said as he turned to watch the basket rise. "What did Granny Bentbone say?"

"Just that she hopes the witch who sent the crows has better luck next time," said Annie.

"She's nasty to the end, isn't she? I must admit, I have to agree with you: those aren't ordinary crows and whoever controls them has to have powerful magic."

"I know, but at least we won't have to worry about what Granny Bentbone might be up to anymore," Annie said.

Liam scratched his head and sighed. "I hope that's true. I'm going to ask my father to have his men keep an eye on this tower just in case."

"It's funny, but now that the crows have done their worst, I'm not really afraid of them. I think I'll ride with you now," said Annie.

"If you're sure," said Liam. When she nodded, he gave her another kiss and left to see what still needed to be done.

After the guards hoisted the old woman up to the window, Liam supervised the dismantling of the pulley and helped the men load the basket and rope into the carriage. Annie untied her mare while Liam and the guards combed the area for anything that could be used to reach the tower window. Although the crows were gone, Annie couldn't shake the feeling that someone was watching her and was relieved when they finally started for Casaway, the home of the royal family of Dorinocco.

CHAPTER 6

THEY APPROACHED Liam's family castle from the east as the sun was setting. Perched atop a hill, the white-stone structure rich with soaring arches and lofty turrets looked too insubstantial to be real. Behind it, the pink-and-orange streaks that colored the evening sky only added to the dreamlike quality.

"It's beautiful," said Annie. "How does it feel to be home again?"

"This never really felt like home, at least not the way you mean it," Liam told her. "This is where I lived with my father, who loved me, and my mother, who didn't. I was happier in the forests and fields than in the castle. I feel more at home when I'm with you, regardless of where we are, than I ever did here."

"But your father has made you his heir. Someday you'll be king of Dorinocco, and this castle will be yours."

"And then it will feel like home because you'll be my queen and live here with me."

Annie could see herself living here with Liam and having a family of their own someday. The thought of it made her feel warm inside, and she smiled, prompting Liam to smile back.

Captain Sterling had ridden ahead, but he returned now, spurring his horse to join Liam and Annie. "Your Highness, the guards are raising the drawbridge. I've called to them, but no one is responding."

"I'll deal with this," said Liam.

Annie urged her horse to keep pace with his, and they arrived at the end of the road together. At the base of the hill, a wide ravine separated the castle from the ground around it. The only way across the ravine was over the drawbridge, which had already been raised halfway.

"Hello, the gate!" Liam called, raising his voice. "Prince Liam orders you to lower the drawbridge."

"Wait!" shouted a voice from the other side of the drawbridge as the rattling of the chains grew silent. "I could have sworn I heard someone calling to us."

"You're imagining things again, Godfrey! Keep going with that winch. The kitchen is serving rabbit stew for supper, and I can almost taste it."

"You know my hearing is better than yours, Thurmont! I tell you, I heard a voice. I'm sure it's not just in my head this time. And it's leftover venison, not rabbit stew."

"Listen, you knuckleheads!" shouted Captain Sterling. "Your prince is waiting for you to lower the drawbridge, and you're talking about filling your bellies! Get this drawbridge down now or I'll personally see that you don't eat supper for a week!"

"We're not letting you in until we know that you are who you say you are. Hold on just a minute." A lone figure emerged from the tower that housed the drawbridge and shuffled across the parapet. It was dusk now, and the remaining light was so dim that Annie couldn't see anything but a dark shape.

"I can't make out a bloomin' thing!" shouted Thurmont. "What's the password for today?"

Another figure joined the first to peer down at the riders. "Even the prince wouldn't know today's password, you fool!" said Godfrey. "We change it every day, and he's been gone for weeks." In a louder voice, he called, "Tell us something only the prince would know!"

"You're Godfrey, son of Meckle, who lives by the old stone bridge!" Liam shouted. "Now lower this drawbridge and let us in!"

"What did he say?" asked Thurmont.

"That he's the prince. Grab hold of your side, and let's get this drawbridge lowered. Our prince is back!"

"Why couldn't he have shown up half an hour ago, before we raised the blasted thing?" Thurmont grumbled as he walked back into the tower.

When the top of the drawbridge finally touched the ground, Liam and Annie started across. Two men came running down the stairs from the room above, joining the guards already in the courtyard. They all wore wide grins when they greeted the prince.

"Welcome back, Your Highness!" said Godfrey.

"You're just in time for supper!" Thurmont added.

&

Feeling tired and grubby, Annie was happy to find a pretty room ready for her and even happier when servants filled a tub with hot water. After bathing, Annie dressed in clean clothes and followed the stream of courtiers heading for the great hall. When she arrived, Liam was already there, seated on the dais with his father.

"Welcome to Dorinocco!" said King Montague as Annie approached the table. "Sit beside Liam. I'm sure he wouldn't want it any other way. My son has been telling me about the witch you left in the tower. I'll be happy to keep an eye on her. Pray tell me, how was your sister's wedding?"

"It was lovely," Annie said as she took her seat. "I'm sure Gwendolyn and Beldegard will be very happy."

"Excellent!" said the king. "At least someone will have a happy marriage. I know I didn't. Speaking of which, here's my lovely wife coming to join us."

Annie turned in her seat as Liam's mother entered

the room. The courtiers, who had been talking and laughing just moments before, grew silent as the queen swept across the floor with armed guards on either side.

"Oh, you're here," she said when she saw Liam. "I wondered what special occasion would make your father let me out of the tower. Did you know that he was keeping me locked away like some kind of criminal? Who does that to his wife, I ask you?"

"That's what you get for trying to take over a friendly kingdom behind my back," said the king.

"I would have filled our coffers and doubled the size of our kingdom if your idiot son hadn't gotten in my way," the queen snarled.

"Good day to you, too, Mother," said Liam.

The queen turned up her nose and looked away.

"Actually, the king of Helmswood locked his wife in the dungeon," said Annie. "I don't think he ever lets her out."

"And did she try to take over a kingdom as well?" asked the queen.

"Actually, she drugged the king and tried to kill his daughter."

"How shocking! And did she succeed?" the queen said, casting a sideways glance at Liam.

"No, fortunately," said Annie.

"Then I don't understand why her husband treated her so severely. It's not as though she actually killed someone or I actually took over a kingdom. I really do think both you and the king of Helmswood over-reacted, Montague. And what you did to my darling Clarence! I shall never forgive you for that! He was such a good boy and so obedient."

"To you, perhaps," said the king. "He was as guilty as you were of trying to steal a neighbor's kingdom."

"He was only trying to help Dorinocco! Look at what you've done to him. I'll probably never see my dear boy again. We both deserved better than this!" The queen turned to Annie and said, "If only you had stayed in your parents' castle as you were supposed to. None of this would have happened if you hadn't inter-fered. And as for you, Liam, if you hadn't helped her, she might never have found a prince to kiss her sister, and we'd be ruling Treecrest right now! You're the one I really blame!"

"Of course you do, Mother," said Liam.

"Enough!" bellowed the king. "From the day Liam was born you've been an unnatural mother to him. Nothing was good enough for Clarence, yet you treated Liam with contempt. Guards, you may escort the queen back to her tower."

"But I haven't had my supper yet!"

"You may eat in your tower," said the king. "There's no need for your presence here to spoil everyone's meal."

The queen rose from her seat in a huff and stormed off the dais with a guard on either side. She was leaving the hall when the king shook his head, saying, "I don't know how I put up with that woman for so many years."

"What was Mother talking about?" said Liam. "What happened to Clarence?"

"I debated banishing him or locking him in the tower with his mother, but he took the decision out of my hands by running off to sea," said the king. "No one has heard from him since."

"I'm sure he'll be back someday," Liam said.

"And up to no good, more than likely," said the king.

Annie was yawning when the king glanced her way. "Although I'd enjoy your company, I believe you need your sleep more than conversation," said the king. "Do you think you'll be able to find your room?"

"Yes, thank you," she told him. "This has been a very trying day."

❧

Annie's bed was comfortable, and she fell asleep the moment her head touched the pillow. At dawn a sudden ruckus outside woke her. Sitting up with a start, she couldn't imagine what was creating such a heartstopping, deafening noise. A sense of dread made her heart pound as she slipped out from under the covers and padded barefoot to the window. When she saw what was outside, she shivered and took a step back. The biggest flock of crows that she had ever seen was circling one of the towers like a thick black cloud. In moments the already unbearable noise grew so loud that she had to stick her fingers in her ears. Then, just as suddenly as it had started, the sound stopped and the swarm of crows flew off in one giant mass.

"What was that about?" she wondered aloud.

Unable to go back to sleep, Annie dressed and left the room, hoping to find Liam and get an early start to Snow White's. A page directed her down the corridor leading past the great hall to a room where the king usually ate his breakfast. Unlike Treecrest's royal family, who ate small morning meals in the great hall when their schedule allowed, Liam's family had a room set aside for the family to dine in. King Montague greeted her warmly when he saw her and gestured for her to sit next to him.

"Did you hear those crows?" she asked, taking a seat.

"I think half the kingdom must have heard those crows," said the king. "They were loud enough to raise the dead. I've never seen a flock that large before."

"I don't know if Liam told you, but two crows followed us to the tower where we left Granny Bent-bone. I'm afraid this might have something to do with them."

The king nodded to the serving girl standing by the door. "They flew off into the woods after making all that noise. We can only hope that they're gone for good."

"Who is gone for good?" Liam asked as he joined them.

"We were talking about the crows," said Annie, looking up as the serving girl set fresh muffins, smoked fish, and porridge laced with honey on the table. They were helping themselves to the food when the queen burst into the room, a pair of guards hurrying to keep up with her.

The king scowled. "Guards, why did you bring her here? I didn't give her permission to join me today."

"I made them bring me," said the queen. "I told them that I had something important to tell you and that it couldn't wait."

"What is it?" the king said, his scowl deepening.

"I'm sure you noticed that a flock of crows came to my tower this morning. They brought me a message from a witch named Terobella," she said, waving a piece of parchment in the air. "She says that if I do something for her, she will see that I am freed from the tower. Here, you can read it for yourself."

The king took the parchment and read the message aloud.

Queen Lenore of Dorinocco,
  If you wish to be freed from the tower and
take control of your kingdom, kill the princess

Annabelle. When I know that this has been
accomplished, my crows will come to your aid.
Terobella

Liam jumped to his feet as soon as Annie's name was
mentioned. Putting a protective arm around the princess, he glared at the queen and said, "Get away from
her, Mother!"

"Do you honestly think I'd tell you about it if I were
actually going to accept the witch's offer?" the queen
said, sounding scornful. "I came here right away to tell
you about it, Montague. I'm not the monster you think
I am. You have to see that now."

"Perhaps," said the king. "Do you know this Terobella?"

The queen shook her head. "No, but I assume that
she's a witch if she can control all those crows."

"Perhaps," said the king. "You may return to the tower.
I'll discuss this with you later."

The queen inclined her head and swept from the
room, casting an exultant look at Liam as she went.

"The only reason she told me is that she hopes to get
in my good graces," said the king. "That woman doesn't
do anything unless she thinks it's to her advantage.
She'd probably accept the offer if she thought she could
trust the witch to keep her promise, but your mother
doesn't trust anyone. Well, son, I think you have a real
problem on your hands. Whoever this Terobella is,
she's obviously strong if she can control all those birds.

It might be better if you and Annabelle stayed with me until we've found out more about this witch. At least you're protected here."

"I can't stay," said Annie. "I need to get to Helmswood and my friend Snow White as soon as possible."

"Who do you suppose this witch Terobella is?" said Liam.

Annie shrugged. "We've met lots of witches, but none named Terobella. I do think I've heard it before, though; I just don't remember where. What I want to know is why someone whom I've never met wants to hurt me."

"That's a very good question," said Liam.

"Do you have any enemies? Do you know if anyone hates you?" the king asked Annie.

"It never occurred to me that I might have enemies, but I'm sure there are lots of people who don't like me. There are all the princes who wanted to marry Gwendolyn, then found out they couldn't because I'd helped Beldegard turn back into a human."

"None of them seemed angry about it, just disappointed," said Liam. "What about the fairies Voracia and Sweetness and Light? I can guarantee that neither of them likes you."

"That's true, but why would they get a witch to help them? If they mean me harm, they would handle it themselves."

"And then there's the dwarf named Cragery, and Snow White's stepmother."

"But Cragery is a squirrel now, and Queen Marissa is locked in her husband's dungeon," said Annie. "Even if they were able to cause trouble, I doubt very much that either one could control a flock of crows."

"Regardless of who it is, the most important thing now is to keep you safe," Liam told her. "We should probably stay here as my father suggested, but"—he held up his hand when she began to protest—"I know you, and you'd never agree to that. We'll just have to take the carriage. I know we were looking forward to riding together, but you'll be safer in the carriage than on horseback. The crows won't be able to reach you in there, not with the bars on the windows."

"I suppose," said Annie. "Although the bars make it feel more like a dungeon cell. At least I won't have to listen to Granny Bentbone ask about my hair."

CHAPTER 7

THE FLOCK OF CROWS started following them the
moment they entered the forest. Annie didn't like riding in the carriage, but she was grateful for the bars
on the windows when the crows landed on the roof
and began pecking. Some well-placed arrows chased
them off, leaving dead crows littering the forest floor.

The group rode on, heading west toward the
bridge that would take them to Grelia, the capital of
Montrose. The remaining crows kept their distance
for a time, with only two or three flying alongside the
carriage. It wasn't until Liam and Captain Sterling
wanted to stop to water the horses that they realized
they had another problem.

"The water's been fouled," said one of the guards,
pulling a thirsty horse back from the pond.

Black feathers floated on the water and bird

droppings streaked the stones at the shore. "I bet the crows did this on purpose," said Liam.

"They probably did," Annie replied, peering out the window. "Is there anywhere else we can water the horses near here?"

Liam shook his head. "We'll keep our eyes open, but I don't know of any place between here and the River Rampant, and that's at least three hours away."

They continued on, sending a pair of guards ahead to scout for water. Eventually one of the men came back to report that they had found a small stream. It wasn't far from the road, but they had to unhitch the horses from the carriage and walk them through the trees. Annie stayed in the carriage with three guards standing watch outside. She was surprised when the men came back only minutes after leaving.

"The crows got there before we could," Liam explained through the window while the men hitched the horses to the carriage again. "They're staying upstream, adding to the mess, so it's not going to wash away any time soon. We tried to fend them off, but there were too many of them."

"Either these are very intelligent birds or someone is controlling everything they do," said Annie. "At least they can't ruin the whole river."

Annie sat back in her seat as the carriage started moving again. The road was so dry that the horses and carriage stirred up a cloud of dust, making it difficult to see anything. She was tempted to close the curtains to keep the dust out, but the day was getting hotter and there was little enough air movement even when the curtains were pulled back.

A shadow flashed by. Nervous, Annie tried to peer out the window. She was afraid of the crows, but she was even more afraid of what their presence there meant. The most Annie could do was negate the magic while she was touching something that had a spell cast on it, like the crow that had brushed against her when she was being lowered from the tower. If only she could see the witch face-to-face!

Men shouted up ahead, and the carriage stopped suddenly, making Annie slide to the edge of her seat.

"Annie, stay inside!" Liam hollered.

Horses screamed and men shouted again, but Annie couldn't tell what was happening. As the dust settled, she tried to look out. All she could see, however, were glimpses of men struggling with something out of sight in front of the carriage.

"What happened?" she cried when Horace hurried past.

"It's quicksand," he said, slowing his horse beside the window. "The captain and Prince Liam are stuck."

Annie's breath caught in her throat. The only way there could be quicksand on a well-traveled, dusty road was if magic had put it there. Opening the door, she slipped outside and peered past the horses pulling the carriage. The ground ahead was flat and smooth, yet it glistened as if it was wet. Most of the guards were on one side of the road or the other, using ropes tied to their saddles to pull loose the two mired horses. Liam and Captain Sterling still sat astride their steeds. The captain's gelding had sunk so far into the quicksand that the horse could no longer move his legs. Liam was trying to calm his stallion, which was thrashing as the men worked to pull him onto solid ground.

Annie was about to run to the quicksand to touch it and end the magic when it occurred to her that removing the magic might not be such a good idea. Without magic, the quicksand would revert to dirt and stone, and the men and horses might be partly buried in the road. At least the quicksand allowed them some sort of movement.

"I'll turn it back into a normal road as soon as you're free, but I can't do it until then," she called to Liam.

The prince's head whipped around when he heard Annie's voice. "I told you to stay inside!"

"Yes, but I have to do something to help!"

"I won't let you put yourself in danger!" Liam shouted. "Go back to the carriage!"

"We almost have you out, Your Highness," said Horace as the guards' horses strained to pull Liam's stallion free. The stallion's front legs were on dry ground now, his labored breathing loud enough to hear from where Annie stood. "One more pull!" shouted the elderly guard.

Suddenly, Liam's horse lurched from the quicksand to take a few steps on shaky legs. Captain Sterling's horse was nearly free as well, his only sign of distress his flaring nostrils and the whites around his eyes.

"Princess, look out!" shouted a guard when a crow swooped toward her.

Annie ducked as an entire flock darkened the sky, their wings beating so loudly that the sound filled the air. Horace and two other guards sprang to protect her, sheltering her body with theirs as they set arrows to their bows and let them loose at the crows.

Wrapping her arms over her head and neck, Annie crouched as the guards shot one arrow after another. She didn't see when the captain's horse was pulled from the quicksand, nor did she see Liam jump from his horse and run around the quicksand to her side.

"Are you all right?" he shouted over the noise of the crows as he crouched down beside her.

Annie cried out and threw her arms around him. "I'm fine if you are," she said.

Liam kissed her and held her close, but only for a moment. "You have to get back in the carriage," he said, and began to pick her up.

"Not yet," Annie told him as she wiggled free. "I have to make the road solid first."

"But the crows—" Liam began.

"The guards can fend them off long enough for me to do this. They've been doing a good job so far. If we hurry, this won't take long."

"I don't like this," said Liam.

"Maybe not," Annie told him. "But you know I have to do it."

After a moment's hesitation, the prince let her go. While Annie bent down to touch the quicksand, Liam, Horace, and three other guards stood watch over her. The instant her finger made contact with the glistening patch of ground, it made a slurping sound and became solid once again.

"I'm getting really tired of this," Annie said as she climbed back into the carriage. "And I don't mean riding in this thing. Have you seen any sign of the witch who controls the crows? She must be around here somewhere."

"No, and the men and I have been watching for her. She may be working from a distance."

"And turning the road into quicksand from a distance, too? Is that even possible?"

A guard led Liam's horse to him and held the reins while the prince remounted. "Anything is possible when magic is involved," Liam told Annie. "Especially for a powerful witch. And that's exactly why you can't take any chances. You have to stay in the carriage until we reach Grelia."

Annie grimaced and glanced past him into the

forest. "I wonder what else the witch is capable of doing."

"I can't imagine, but I'm afraid we'll probably find out." The carriage started rolling, and Liam rode beside it so he could talk to Annie through the window.

"I never thought I'd say this, but why can't I find a fairy godmother when I need one?" said Annie. "I don't like magic; I just think that sometimes it would be useful to have some—like right now. I've been thinking about this. There are two kinds of magic people can use against you. There's the kind where a spell is cast at a person and can affect her directly, or the kind that affects something or someone in the person's surroundings. I can handle the first kind because the spell bounces right off me. It's the second kind that can cause me problems, and this witch seems to know it. I can't stop her from using magic when she turns it on someone or something else. It would be handy if I knew someone who could."

❧

The thirsty horses sensed the river before the people did. Perking up their ears, they trotted down the last bit of road; it was all their riders could do to keep them from going straight to the water's edge, where large, jumbled rocks could easily break a horse's legs. Although the river was turbulent, the horses pawed the ground, anxious to drink from it.

"There's a path over here!" shouted the captain. "Bring your horses down one at a time."

Annie waited impatiently as the men unhitched the horses and took them to the river. Her back was sore, and her entire body was stiff from spending the day in the small enclosed space. She envied the riders the chance to stretch their legs and drink.

She was peering out the window when she discovered that if she moved to the other side of her seat, she could see part of the bridge. It was a wooden structure with massive pillars that held it high above the water so that small boats could pass underneath. Annie was admiring the bridge when Liam appeared at the window. "The crows are perched in the trees on the other side of the river. It's almost as if they know where we're going. Ah, good, the last horse is finished. We'll be leaving in a few minutes."

When the carriage began moving again, Annie slid closer to the window, wanting to see the view from the top of the bridge. They had traveled nearly halfway across when the carriage shook and lurched to the side. The riders both in front and behind the carriage shouted. Annie grabbed hold of the bars on the window to keep from falling to the floor. She heard the sound of cracking wood, and suddenly the end of the bridge was a mass of splintered logs crashing into the river around the falling carriage.

The carriage plummeted, turning as it fell so that it

landed on its side. The force of the fall wrenched Annie's shoulder, and she let go of the bars as water poured through the window. Not knowing how deep the water was, she held her breath just as the carriage lurched again and slammed into the riverbed. The side that was now on top was above the water, so she pushed off from the bottom and shoved the door open.

Annie heaved herself out of the carriage and stopped to look around. The horses that had been pulling the carriage were floundering in the water, the swingletree that connected their traces to the carriage having snapped on impact. One of the guards who had been driving had already managed to get on the back of the lead horse and was trying to turn it to shore. The other man waved at Annie, then dove into the water beside the carriage with a knife in his hand. Seconds passed before the head of the dappled gray mare burst out of the water, snorting and puffing, her eyes wide in fear. The man emerged a moment later to follow the swimming horse to shore.

Men and horses were struggling to the water's edge, singly and together. When Annie looked for Liam, she saw that his horse was climbing out of the river without a rider. Her heart seemed to stop for a moment, but then she saw him still in the water, swimming toward her.

"Are you all right?" he asked as he drew close enough that she could hear him.

"I'm fine," she said, ignoring a twinge in her shoulder. "What about you?"

"Never better," he said, but his expression was grim. "What happened?"

"A perfectly good bridge that my father inspects every six months collapsed just as we happened to be crossing it."

"It must be that witch again," Annie said. "How is everyone else?"

They both turned to watch the last of the horses leave the water farther downstream, where the current had carried them. Men were already gathered on the shore to lead them to the rest of the group. "It looks as if they're all accounted for. Stay here. I'll be right back. And I mean it, Annie. Don't move from this spot."

"All right!" she said, holding up her hands. "I won't go anywhere!"

Liam dove into the water beside the carriage and came up a moment later shaking his head. "The axle is broken. This carriage is worthless now."

"Then I guess I'll ride horseback the rest of the way," said Annie.

"Try not to look so disappointed," Liam said, smiling.

Unlike most princesses, Annie knew how to swim. She and Liam reached the riverbank at the same time, and climbed out just as Horace came slogging across the shore leading Annie's mare. "Your Highness," Horace said to Annie. "Your mare is sound enough to ride— just needs a bit of a rest is all. She was mighty scared, but she'll calm down in a bit, you'll see."

The mare danced to the side, skittery from the accident, as Horace led her to where the other horses had been tethered.

"I'm going to send the carriage drivers back to my father to tell him about the bridge," said Liam. "The first order of business, however, is to get a fire going. We can make camp beside the river tonight and get an early start in the morning."

"The carriage!" cried one of the men on the shore.

Annie and Liam both looked toward the river. Whatever had been holding the carriage in place had given way, allowing the current to carry it bumping and tumbling past them and out of sight.

"I think my tent was in there," said Annie. "This day just keeps getting better. How long do you think we'll have to travel to reach Grelia tomorrow?"

"If we're lucky, just a few hours, but there's no saying how long it will take if we have another day like today."

"Great!" said Annie. "Because I'm sure the witch and her crows will do their best to make it perfect."

❧

Annie sat shivering on a log, watching a guard coax a flame from flint and tinder while two others kept the crows away. The dry kindling caught, and soon the logs were crackling as flames licked up their sides. From the moment Annie and her companions had climbed out of the river, the crows had pestered them. As the flames spread, however, the birds flew off, landing in trees a good distance away.

Reaching her hands toward the fire, Annie let its warmth soak into her. Her clothes dried quickly, and soon her face was uncomfortably hot, so she turned around to dry the clothes on her back and warm the rest of her.

"It seems that someone thought it would be a good idea to store all the tents in the compartment under your seat in the carriage," Liam told her as he sat down. "The carriage is lost now, so we'll be sleeping under the stars tonight."

"We should be fine as long as we keep the fire going," said Annie. "The crows don't seem to like it."

"Half of our supplies were in the carriage, too, so we'll have to make do with what's left."

"Some of the men are fishing," Annie said, pointing toward the river. "If we're lucky, we'll have fresh fish for supper."

"Now, Annie," said Liam, "I know how much you want to help Snow White, but it's much too dangerous. This witch isn't going to give up. If you won't return home, I think you should remain in Grelia when we get there. You'd be safer in King Berwick's castle than on the road. I'm sure Beldegard's parents would love to have you stay with them. Let me find a way to take care of the witch, and then you can go home safely. Snow White would understand."

Annie shook her head. "I have to go to Helmswood now. Snow White asked for my help, and I'm not about to turn her down. Besides, someone was trying to kill me before we ever left Treecrest. I don't think I'd be any safer in a castle than I am with you and all these guards to protect me."

"I didn't think you'd give up, but I'm still worried," said Liam. "By the way, your cheeks are flushed. Don't get overheated sitting here."

"I'm enjoying the warmth of the fire and sitting still instead of bumping down the road," said Annie. "I think the witch did me a favor when she made the bridge collapse. I don't know if I could have ridden in that carriage any longer."

"You may miss it after a few hours in the saddle tomorrow," said Liam.

"Maybe," said Annie. "But at least now I'll be able to ride next to you."

The three guards who had been fishing came trudging toward the fire, each carrying a string of fish. With so many eager hands to help, their catch was soon cleaned and sizzling on sticks held over the flames. Annie was hungry, but she wasn't the only one who couldn't wait for the fish to cool; nearly everyone burned their fingers when the cooked fish were finally handed out.

The sun had set when they organized the watch, and the travelers who weren't due to stand guard settled down to sleep around the fire. Annie found comfort in the knowledge that the guards who were taking turns watching over the camp were also going to keep the fire stoked. With the fire holding the crows at bay, she might actually get a good night's rest.

Annie had been asleep for only a few hours when the sound of men talking in muted voices woke her. She was half listening, half dozing when she heard one of them say "Wolves." Suddenly, she was wide awake.

"I tell you, I saw red eyes watching me from those trees over there," one of the guards whispered to another.

"I don't see anything," said the second guard.

"They were there, I tell you. Look! There they are!"

"I don't see anything. Were you staring into the fire again? Because if you were ... Wait! You're right! And over there! And there! Captain!" called the guard. "It looks as if a pack of wolves is coming at us from every side."

In an instant, all the men were on their feet with weapons in their hands.

"Did you say wolves?" asked Liam, peering into the trees. "No one has seen a wolf around here for—never mind. There's one now. Annie, get behind me! And this time, please listen!"

Annie scrambled toward Liam, wishing she had thought to arm herself before she'd gone to sleep. She glanced back at the twang of bowstrings. Guards were shooting at the wolves, a job made more difficult in the dancing light and shadows of the fire.

"Save your arrows!" Liam shouted as more than one went astray. "We're running low, and you'll need them to fend off the crows tomorrow."

Dropping their bows, the guards unsheathed their swords and stood poised for the attack. As the wolves moved out of the shadows and into the firelight, Annie could see that something wasn't quite right. Instead of attacking, they began to act very strangely. One hopped a few feet and stopped to look around. Another took one look at the guards and began trying to burrow under the old leaves on the forest floor. A third ran to a tree and scrabbled at the trunk as if trying to climb it. The others took a few steps, looking more frightened than menacing. Not one of the wolves actually turned on the humans.

"What's going on?" asked Annie.

"I don't know," said Liam. "They look like wolves, but they aren't acting like them."

"It's another of the witch's tricks!" cried Horace.

Liam nodded. "They look as if they don't want to be here, but something is making them confront us."

"Perhaps it's a compulsion that the witch placed on them," said Captain Sterling.

The wolf that had tried to hop toward them made another awkward attempt, but his paws went out from under him and he sprawled face-first in the leaves.

"Liam, when was the last time you saw a wolf?" Annie asked.

"I haven't seen a real wolf since I traveled to the Misty Mountains," said Liam. "But there was that man the dwarf turned into a wolf. Do you remember him?"

"Yes," Annie replied. "He told us that when he first turned into a wolf, he didn't know how to act like one or even walk like one. It looks as if these wolves are having the same problem."

"So you think they're men?" asked the captain.

"Not really," Annie said. "But we'd know for sure if we could catch one."

"If they're not really wolves, I can catch you one, Your Highness," said Horace.

"You're too old!" cried one of the younger guards. "Just leave it to us able-bodied men!"

"Hah!" cried Horace, setting his sword on the ground so he could dig in his knapsack for a piece of rope. "I'll have one of these pretend wolves hog-tied before you can say your auntie's name three times backward. Get out of my way and let an expert handle this."

Four of the youngest guards grinned and reached for their own ropes. In just moments, the five men were chasing the wolves around the fire, trying to snare the animals, which, strangely, were unable to move very fast.

"Got one!" Horace shouted just as a younger guard tackled another wolf. The two men dragged the wolves toward Annie, who hurried to meet them partway. While Horace held his captive still, Annie laid her hand on the animal's side. The change began immediately, and in less than a minute, a rabbit lay where the wolf had been, its eyes wide in terror. When Annie took her hand away, Horace let go and the rabbit hopped off into the forest.

"Can you see what this one is, too, Your Highness?" the other guard asked. "He's a wiggly fellow, but he hasn't tried to bite me even once."

At Annie's touch, the wolf faded away as the animal's true self emerged. It was a chipmunk and was so small that Annie could have held it in one hand. When Annie and the guard both stepped back, the little creature scurried into the underbrush.

"I don't think this spell was meant to last," said Annie, glancing at the other animals, all of which were also looking less wolflike. A moment later a deer bounded toward the woods, a raccoon climbed a tree, and a skunk ran off, its tail in the air.

"Or the witch isn't as powerful as we thought she was," Liam replied. "Either way, that was a close call, but they're gone now, so I think we should try to get some sleep."

"A close call because they weren't really wolves?" Annie asked as the returned to their places by the fire.

"No," Liam said. "Because that skunk could have done some real damage if it hadn't run off just then!"

CHAPTER 8

THEY SPOTTED THE CAPITAL CITY of Grelia after only a few hours of riding the next day. A high stone wall enclosed most of the city, but Annie could see the castle towering above it when they were still miles away.

"Beldegard grew up in Grelia, and he told me all about it," said Liam. "It has one of the oldest castles in all the kingdoms. The wall you see is the newest. It dates back only a few hundred years. There are other walls inside from when the city was older and smaller. There are three or four walls altogether, but the guards close only the outside gates at night."

"Do you think King Berwick and his family have returned home yet?"

"Probably. I think they left the same day we did. The princes who want to court Snow White were traveling with them, so the question is, did all the princes get here yet? Some of them are slow travelers."

"Especially Andreas," said Annie. "Although the thought of winning Snow White's hand might have made them move a little faster."

They rode past prosperous farms for a time, which eventually gave way to cottages and even a market outside the city walls. The guards standing on both sides of the open gate into the city were alert but polite, letting them through as soon as they identified themselves.

The roads inside the first gate were broad and straight, but when they passed through the second gate, the roads became narrower and angled off in different directions. After the third gate, the roads became a maze they might have gotten lost in if Horace hadn't known his way around.

"I was born in Grelia," Annie overheard him telling another guard. "My family lived here until I was twelve. That's when they moved to Treecrest. My dad got a job on one of the linder tree farms up north. My sisters still live there with their families, but my aunts and uncles and cousins all live in Grelia. Except my nephew Niko. He lives in . . . ah, good! There's the gate," said Horace, interrupting himself as he pointed to an ornate archway with a room above and a row of narrow buildings on either side.

They were riding under the arch when Horace gestured to the wall behind the buildings. "That's actually the curtain wall for the castle. There's a huge black pot filled with oil kept just above us and logs ready for lighting under the pot should an invader get this far. My dad had buddies in the castle guards, and they let him take me on a tour once."

As they entered the courtyard beyond the gate, Annie was reminded of her home. The layout of the outbuildings seemed to be the same, although these were older.

"Your Highnesses, you'll want to go up those stairs right there while we take care of the horses and I show the captain to the guards' quarters," said Horace.

The guards rode off as Annie and Liam started up the stairs. "Don't you get the feeling that Horace thinks he's in charge sometimes?" Annie asked Liam.

"True. Especially on this trip. I think he believes it's his personal responsibility to take care of you, but then I think we've all claimed that job," he said, giving her hand a squeeze.

A thin man wearing a gold medallion on a chain waited at the top of the stairs. He bowed when he saw them, and immediately began to herd them through the door that led into the great hall. "Welcome to Grelia! I'm Stanford, the royal steward. You are probably hungry after your trip. The royal family eats together in a smaller hall during the day. They just sat down for their midday meal and are anxious that you join them. This way, if you please."

"Wonderful!" said Annie. They had eaten very little

that morning, and her stomach had been rumbling so loudly that she was afraid everyone could hear it.

High windows filled the great hall with light, making it a pleasant room. A little boy dressed as a page ran by with a small dog barking at his heels. Two girls dressed in the fine clothes of noblemen's daughters sat side by side, smiling behind their hands as they eyed a handsome young man at a nearby table. A group of middle-aged women sat gossiping over nearly empty tankards, the scraps of their just-eaten meal in front of them. It was a friendly place, and everyone seemed content. When they saw the steward leading Annie and Liam through the hall, they watched with curious eyes, and more than one smiled and nodded.

"I liked Beldegard's parents when we met them before the wedding, but you need to see what a person's home life is like before you really know them," Annie told Liam under her breath. "People here seem happy. I think Gwennie married into a good family."

"I could have told you that," said Liam. "Beldegard told me a lot about them."

"Right this way, Your Highnesses," the steward said, leading them into a corridor, where he opened one of the first doors. "Please let me know if I can be of service in any way." The steward bowed again, but Annie and Liam were already peering into the room.

Although the room wasn't nearly as big as the great hall, it was still quite large. Only one of the three round tables was occupied, and even that table wasn't full. Annie spotted King Berwick, who was as big as his son Beldegard, sitting beside Queen Nara and their two daughters. The princes Cozwald, Emilio, and Andreas were also there, but neither Maitland nor Digby were present.

Everyone looked up as Annie and Liam entered the room. "Oh, good!" cried Tyne. "Now you can see what we were talking about, Mother. Anyone who gets near Annie starts to look ordinary!"

Queen Nara smiled weakly, then told her daughter in a quiet voice, "It isn't polite to point that sort of thing out."

"But she was just saying—" Willa began.

"Willa!" her mother snapped.

King Berwick smiled indulgently at his daughters, then glanced at Annie and Liam while gesturing to two empty chairs. "Come join us. There's plenty of room!"

"We expected you to arrive yesterday," Cozwald said as Annie and Liam took their seats.

"We ran into a few . . . delays," said Liam.

Annie noticed that Queen Nara was leaning down to talk to Tyne. The twins were both looking in Annie's direction.

Annie made herself turn to Emilio, who was seated beside her. "When did you arrive?"

"Yesterday afternoon. We would have gotten here sooner, but one of the twins was carriage-sick and we had to keep stopping. I understand you were going to drop the old witch off at the tower. How did that go?"

"Not as smoothly as we would have liked, but she's there now," said Annie. "Where are Maitland and Digby?"

A serving girl came by to offer a platter of smoked sausage. "I assume they're still in bed," said Emilio. "I haven't seen either one all morning."

Annie forced herself not to turn around when she heard the twins giggling. "Digby was up late again last night," said Andreas. "I went to ask him if he wanted to join us for breakfast, but he was feeling under the weather. Maitland wasn't there when I stopped by his room."

When Andreas turned toward the queen as if she would know where her son might be, Queen Nara sighed and set down her fork. "Maitland didn't want it to be general knowledge yet, but I told him I wouldn't lie for him. He left early this morning. He's on his way to Helmswood."

"He left without us?" said Cozwald. "I thought we were traveling together."

"Apparently he wanted a head start with the princess Snow White," Emilio said.

Andreas pushed his chair away from the table and stood. "Then we should leave right away. Maitland has already met the princess. He doesn't need an even greater advantage."

"But Princess Annabelle and Prince Liam just arrived. Surely they'll need time to rest," said the queen.

"I'm ready to go if you are, Annie," said Liam.

Annie sighed. "We can go, but I really would like to eat first."

"You can finish eating while I send word to the captain that we'll be moving on sooner than expected. May I trouble you for some provisions?" he asked the king.

"Of course," said King Berwick. "Annabelle is family now that my son is married to her sister. Is there anything else you need?"

"We are short of arrows," Liam replied.

"Really?" said Cozwald. "Since I assume that you set out from Treecrest well supplied, you must have run into some trouble. What happened?"

Liam glanced at Annie, then back to the prince. "We had a run-in with some crows. They've followed us most of the way."

"What kind of crows?" asked Willa.

"I think they're probably ordinary crows," said Annie, "but a witch is controlling them."

"Really?" said Tyne. "What does the witch look like? Do you know her name?"

"We haven't seen her yet, but we think her name is Terobella," said Liam.

The king and the queen exchanged glances. "We've heard of her," said King Berwick. "She used to live in Montrose, but she moved away not too long ago. If she's involved, you should be careful. She's got a reputation for being truly malicious. Liam, perhaps you and I should take a look in my armory and see what else you might need."

"And I'll go see about Digby," Emilio said. "Under the weather or not, it wouldn't be right to leave him behind."

"Plus it wouldn't hurt to have another man along," said Andreas. "I'm pretty good with a bow myself. I'd like to go with you to your armory, if you don't mind, Your Majesty."

"Of course you may join us," said the king. When a serving girl offered him fresh bread, he shook his head and turned back to Liam. "Would you like some of my knights to travel with you?"

"I don't think that's necessary," said Liam. "We brought guards with us, and with the princes and their attendants added to our number, we should have plenty of eyes to keep watch and strong fighters if we need them."

"Can we come, too?" asked Tyne. "I've never seen a real witch."

"And I hope you never will," said her mother. "At least not an evil one like Terobella."

≈

They left Grelia a few hours later with Liam and Cozwald in the lead. Digby, who still wasn't feeling well, started out beside them but soon drifted farther back in the line. They formed a large party now, as each of the princes had brought at least two attendants with him. Like the guards who had come with them, both Annie's and Liam's horses were outfitted for travel, so no one gave them a second glance, but the other princes were all dressed like royalty and rode warhorses wearing their most impressive trappings. Waving, cheering crowds gathered in the road before the party reached the second gate. Riding farther back in the line, Annie could see how each prince reacted. Andreas was friendly, waving back to the people who waved to him. Emilio looked as if the attention made him uncomfortable, but Cozwald acted as if it was his due. When Annie looked behind her, she saw that Digby was enjoying himself, preening when pretty girls called out to him. Their progress through the city was slower than before, and Annie was relieved when they finally passed through the last gate.

The road from the castle led across an open field, but they could see the forest less than a mile away, looking like a vast green wall. Heading west to Helmswood meant that they'd be traveling through thick forest most of the way. Although Annie usually enjoyed forests, she wasn't looking forward to spending so much time in an unfamiliar one while a witch was after her. Even before they reached the trees, she looked around, waiting for something to happen, but the birds kept their distance and the road stayed solid beneath the horses' hooves. As the cool shade of the trees finally engulfed them, Annie took a deep breath, trying to calm her jittery nerves.

ॐ

After a time, the road began to angle uphill and curve to the left. Although nothing unexpected appeared in the curve of the road, Annie wouldn't let herself relax. When the ground on the left began to rise sharply, she feared that a boulder might come tumbling down the hill just as they were passing by. Noticing that the ground on the right descended in a gentle incline, she half expected a wild creature to come tearing up the hill to launch itself at them. She even looked suspiciously at the tiny stream trickling down what had become a sheer rock wall, but the most surprising thing she saw was a large woodpecker flitting from one tree to another.

Liam had been talking to the other princes, telling them about everything that had happened to them on their trip. When he finally rode down the line to join Annie, he looked tired and worried, but she was happy to see him.

"I keep expecting the crows to attack or some strange beast to jump out of the forest," she said. "The anticipation is killing me!"

"I know what you mean," said Liam. "The witch

probably knows it, too, and is doing it on purpose. She'll hold back while we feel more and more edgy, then the moment we let our guard down, she'll throw something new at us."

"I wonder what it will be this time," Annie said, glancing over her shoulder.

"I'm sure we'll find out soon enough," said Liam. "Uh-oh. Digby is dozing in his saddle and is about to fall off. I'll be back in a little while."

Annie turned to watch Liam ride down the line to Digby. The sleeping prince was swaying precariously and looked as if he was going to tumble to the ground at any moment. Annie was still turned in her saddle when a bolt of lightning ripped through the clear blue sky and hit a tree at the uphill side of the road. There was a loud *CRACK!* and the tree fell across their path, sending a cloud of dust and debris into the air.

Annie calmed her frightened mare and looked around to see if anyone needed help. Although the warhorses did nothing more than get a little shifty-footed, some of the attendants' horses were more high-strung. Andreas's squire was flung from his horse when it screamed and reared, but the young man was unhurt and the horse was soon caught and quieted.

"A tree just fell down," Horace called as he rode back to join her. "Best stay right here, Your Highness, until we find out the cause. No storm, just a lightning bolt. I'd say it was magic again."

Horace's gelding sidestepped out of the way when Liam's horse tore past, slowing only long enough for Liam to shout, "Annie, stay there!"

She stayed where she was for a few minutes, but when nothing else happened and no one came to tell her what was going on, she started toward the front of the line. Horace followed her, protesting all the way to the fallen tree. It was an old tree, with a trunk at least five feet around, and it stretched all the way across the road, jutting over a drop-off on the other side.

"Now what?" she asked as Liam caught sight of her.

"The next time I'm tempted to tell you to stay anywhere, I might as well save my breath," Liam said, looking angrier than she'd ever seen him. "Don't you understand? A witch is trying to kill you, and we're all trying to stop her. When I ask you to stay where you are, it's to keep you safe, yet you insist on disregarding my orders!"

"Orders?" said Annie, feeling the color rise in her cheeks. "I'm not one of your men who you can order around!"

"No, you're my future wife, and I won't let you get hurt!" Liam sat back on his horse and took a deep breath as he glanced at the fallen tree. When he turned to Annie again, he looked calmer and no longer sounded angry. "All I'm doing is trying to keep you safe, so will you please listen to me? A tree has blocked the road, and as you can see it's too big to move. We don't have a saw to cut it, and it's too high for most of these horses to jump, so we're going to have to go around it. However, the rocks just past the tree make it impossible to get back to the road for quite a distance. This tree didn't just happen to fall here. It was meant to force us off this road and down this hill. I've sent two men to scout the area to see what lies in that direction. We'll make our decision when they return."

"Is that them now?" Annie asked, peering at two shapes moving toward them from the shadows under the trees.

"We didn't see anything unusual," the men called as they drew closer. "The ground gets a bit marshy, but there are ways around it."

"If you think it's a trap, maybe we should go back and find another road," said Cozwald.

Andreas frowned. "I say we go downhill. Maitland already has a head start. I don't want it to get any bigger, and who knows how much time we'd lose if we looked for another road."

"Horace, are you familiar with this area?" Annie asked him.

The old guard shrugged. "A little. It's safe enough—no trolls or dangerous beasts, if that's what you're thinking."

"We might as well go this way," said Liam. "As we've already seen, the witch can turn even the most innocent stretch of road into something dangerous. We'll probably end up facing her vile magic again, no matter where we go."

"Do you see any crows?" Annie asked Liam as the riders turned their horses to the downhill slope.

"Two in front of us and two behind," Liam said, glancing back over his shoulder. "They've been with us since we reached the forest."

"Maybe they're staying back because they're afraid of you. You reduced their numbers by quite a few."

"I doubt that would make much of a difference to the witch," said Liam. "I think she's saving them for something."

❧

Both Liam and Horace kept their horses close to Annie's as they made their way down the slope. They began to look for a way back to the road as soon as they could, but Liam had been right when he said that the rocks made it impossible. Although they tried to ride side by side, some of the trees grew too close together, forcing them to go single file. Annie didn't realize that they'd reached the marshy area until her horse's hooves began splashing through water.

"You said there were some ways around this," Liam said, turning to the guards who had scouted ahead.

"There are, Your Highness. At least there were," said one of the men. "The thing is...I don't see them now. Do you?" he asked the other guard.

"I could have sworn there was a path right over there," said the second guard. "But those trees...I don't remember seeing them."

"And I thought there was an old stump next to a path over there, but the stump seems to be gone, and there doesn't appear to be a path."

"We know where the road is," said Cozwald. "We'll just head back that way and—"

Cozwald gasped, and everyone turned to look behind them. Trees now blocked the way they had just come, and water covered much of what had been dry ground only moments before. Something created ripples in the water, and one of the horses in the back of the line shied away from the water's edge.

Digby snorted. "You're all a bunch of ninnies! That's just an illusion. Nothing can move trees like that, and that water isn't real. Watch. I'll show you."

When his horse was reluctant to approach the water, the prince urged it on with spurs. A few steps and the horse's hooves were wet; another step and it was up to its hocks in water.

"Keep going, you useless beast!" Digby shouted, digging his spurs into the horse's sides. The horse plunged forward, and the water covered its legs.

Suddenly, long, snaky vines whipped from the murky depths, wrapping themselves around the horse's neck. The horse tried to rear, but the vines held it down as even more vines wrapped around Digby's arms and legs. Eyes wide, ears pinned back, the horse tried to thrash free, but the vines only grew tighter. Although Digby struggled to pull his arms loose, his efforts were just as useless.

"Isn't anyone going to help me?" Digby shouted, his face turning red.

The two closest guards jumped from their horses' backs and ran toward the water, their swords in their hands. The moment they entered the water, vines began to wrap around their legs, holding them in place while other vines rose up to pull them below the water's surface.

Liam, Cozwald, and Andreas were all beginning to dismount when Annie slid from her mare's back.

"No, Annie!" Liam shouted, but she had already thrown her reins to Horace and was running toward the struggling men. Liam jumped to the ground and started after her. Before he could reach her, however, Annie entered the water, which began to drain away, leaving the guards gasping for air. When she touched the first guard, the vine holding him down shriveled and fell off. She reached for the second, and he was soon free as well.

"What about me?" shouted Digby.

As Annie strode toward Digby, the last of the water disappeared and the vines fell away at her touch. Digby's horse shivered and grew calmer. Brushing past Annie,

Liam reached for the horse's reins and led it back to its place in line.

"You didn't listen to me again," he said in a quiet voice as he walked Annie to her horse.

"And everyone is fine because I didn't listen to you!" said Annie, not bothering to keep her voice down. "Yes, there are times I really can't defend myself from certain kinds of things, but there are times when I'm the *only* one who can actually help, and that's when you have to let me go! I know you want to keep me safe. I also know that sometimes it's up to me to keep *you* safe! So don't try to stop me when I'm doing what I actually *can* do! Now," she said, turning to the two guards who had first scouted the area, "where did you say those paths were?"

"There was a stump over there and a path beside it," said the man, pointing to a clump of grass.

Retrieving her mare's reins from Horace, Annie headed straight for the grass while the other riders re-formed their line behind her. She was only feet away when the stump reappeared with a deer path running past it. "Stay close behind me," she said, turning to the men. "If the path disappears again, stay where you are and I'll come back for you."

The deer path wasn't straight and didn't head directly back to the road, but it did lead to drier ground, and eventually Annie saw the road to her left.

Liam and Horace helped her clear a way through some underbrush, and they were soon back on the road, tired and dirty, but relieved.

"We have company," Liam said as the rest of the princes straggled onto the road.

"I see that," said Annie. She tilted her head back to gaze up at the flock of crows watching from the branches overhead. "It's funny, but I'm starting to get used to them. I'm really not as afraid of them as I was before."

"They're still dangerous," Liam reminded her.

"I know," said Annie. "But so am I."

CHAPTER 9

THEY REACHED SNOW WHITE'S CASTLE a few hours later. Annie had just crossed the drawbridge and reined her horse to a stop when a white shape shot across the courtyard, barking. "Dog!" Annie cried. She slid off her mare so she could crouch down and throw her arms around the shaggy dog's neck. A wet tongue licked the side of her face while the animal's wiggly body vibrated with joy. "How have you been? Are you happy here?" asked Annie. When the dog didn't answer, Annie pulled away and looked her in the eyes. Dog's tongue lolled out of the side of her mouth so that she almost seemed to be laughing. "Oh, right! I forgot." Annie patted the dog's head and stepped away. "You can't talk when I'm touching you."

Dog's tail wagged like a pendulum. "I'm glad you're here," the animal said in a rush. "Snow White told me you were coming. I've been waiting here for you every day." She looked past Annie to all the princes and guards. "If they came with you, they can come in. This is a very big place. It has lots of rooms. Good smells, too. I'm taking you to see Snow White. She's been waiting for you. Just you, though. The rest have to go somewhere else."

"All right," said Annie. "Lead the way." When she grabbed her mare's reins, she felt a tug on her hem and looked down.

Dog gave her a reproachful look and backed away so she could talk again. "The horse can't go with us. Snow White doesn't let horses in the castle."

"But I was just...," Annie began. "Um, never mind." Handing her reins to Liam, she shrugged and said, "I'll find you later." Then she turned to follow Dog.

The last time Annie had been in the castle, Snow White's stepmother had been ruling for many years. The evil queen had neglected the castle as she'd plotted and schemed, spending little money on the buildings and letting the furnishings get rundown and dirty. Although it had been only a few weeks since Snow White had returned home and her stepmother had been locked away, repairs had already begun, and the floors and windows looked cleaner. Even now, maids scrubbed walls while seamstresses repaired tapestries.

One thing didn't seem to have changed, however. Everyone, from the lowest servant to the highest noble, had looked frightened during Annie's last visit. The unpredictable evil queen had made them wary of doing even the simplest thing that might displease her. Annie had been sure that Snow White's presence would change that and was dismayed to find that it hadn't. Footmen kept their eyes averted when Annie looked their way. A noblewoman hurried off when Annie gave her a friendly smile. When Annie glanced at a maid carrying an armload of linens, the girl ducked her head and scurried around a corner, looking so frightened that Annie almost called after her.

Confused, Annie followed Dog down the corridor and up a narrow set of stairs. She was used to people avoiding her because she might take away their magic, but this was different. Although the inhabitants of the castle seemed fearful, she didn't think it had anything to do with her.

"This is it," Dog finally said. "Snow White's room."

Dog raised her paw and tapped on the door three times. She was about to tap again when the door opened. Snow White was there, a smile lighting her face when she saw Annie.

"You came!" she cried, pulling Annie into the room. "Thank you for bringing her, Dog. Go tell the cook that I said you should have an extra-big bone!"

Dog walked off, her tail wagging again, as Snow White shut the door.

"Dog is such a dear creature, but she doesn't know how to keep secrets, and there are things I need to tell you that I don't want everyone to know," said Snow White. "Come sit over here so we can talk."

As Annie sat down on the window seat, Snow White began to fidget with a tassel on a cushion. "Cat is here as well," she finally said, glancing at Annie. "He stops by to see me every few days. I think he's just checking up on me to see if I'm all right."

"Why wouldn't you be?" asked Annie. "Snow White, what's going on?"

Snow White stood abruptly and began to pace. "I don't know what to do. You know that Father locked my stepmother, Marissa, in the dungeon when he learned that she had been putting drugs in his drink and trying to kill me. Just a few days after you and Liam left, she escaped. We still don't know how she did it, but we think she must have had help. Father is afraid that Marissa still wants to kill me. Now he's gotten the idea that if I were to marry, my prince would whisk me away to his castle and I would finally be safe from her." Snow White was wringing her hands when she turned back to Annie. "Isn't that the craziest idea you've ever heard?"

"Well...," Annie began.

"In the meantime, Father has doubled the guards. Everyone is terrified that Marissa will come back. Knowing how much she likes disguises, some think she may be here already."

"Oh my...," Annie said.

"Father sent out word to the neighboring kingdoms that I'm looking for a husband! Can you believe that? Next he'll be flying banners at the local jousting tournaments reading 'Come one, come all! Feast your eyes on the desperate princess!' I can't believe he's done this to me!"

"So," said Annie, "are you more upset because a crazy woman may be coming to kill you, or because your father was a little indiscreet about your availability?"

"Both! Although I guess the killing one is worse.... But not by much!"

"Have you heard from any princes yet?" Annie asked.

"Four. Three who I've never heard of before they arrived yesterday with their attendants, and then Maitland showed up a few hours ago. He's been sending me messages and flowers, but I couldn't bring myself to see him. Not after the last time he was here and he told his friends how much he wanted to rule my kingdom. Where is the romance in that? I want to be loved for myself, not the land my father rules or the castle we live in or the gold in our treasury. And I'm sure that after Father's announcement, that's all the other princes are going to see. Now Father is making me choose among these four princes, and he says he wants me to do it in a week's time. The thing is, I don't have any idea how to begin!"

"You actually have a few more princes to choose from. Four more came with me. There's Andreas,

Cozwald, his cousin Emilio, and Digby," Annie said, ticking them off on her fingers. "So with the four who are already here, you have eight princes."

"That just makes it worse!" wailed Snow White.

"You don't have any idea how you're going to choose?" Annie asked.

"None. I've spent all my time thinking about it, but nothing has come to me," Snow White declared. "I know some princesses send their suitors on quests, but I don't have time for that. Not if Father is giving me only a week!"

Annie thought her friend looked close to tears. "Maybe I can help. What are you looking for in a husband?"

"That's what makes it so hard," said Snow White, wringing her hands again. "They're all handsome, and they are all talented in one thing or another, and they all have excellent manners."

"And those are the most important things to you?" asked Annie.

"Well, not really," Snow White said, beginning to pace again. "He has to be honest, and brave. He also has to be compassionate. Oh, and more than anything, he has to love me for myself."

"Those are all very good traits. And how do you think you can learn if any of those things are true of these princes?"

"A contest?" asked Snow White.

"That could work," said Annie. "Do you have a quill, some ink, and a piece of parchment? I think it's time to make a list."

"I have them right here," said Snow White, gesturing toward a table in the center of the room. "You know, a contest might actually be fun."

"For us, maybe," said Annie, "but the prince who really wants to win is going to have to work hard. It may not be as much fun for him. You realize, of course, that no man is going to show you what he's really like in a contest. They'll all try to impress you with their best behavior. The princes might be very different once they relax and you really get to know them."

"I'm sure you're right," said Snow White. "I grew up in a house with seven men. None of them tried to impress me, but I do know what I don't want. I don't want a man who thinks it's funny to talk about bodily functions or who doesn't like to bathe."

"Ick!" said Annie. "How about a man who thinks mean jokes are funny? Or who loves his mother more than he loves you?"

"Or one who loves his horse more than me!" Snow White said with a laugh. "Oh, I've thought of something else I do want. I want to marry a good kisser. I've never kissed a man, except on the cheek, and I want my first real kiss to be spectacular!"

"I don't think we can make that part of the contest," said Annie.

"I know," Snow White said, though she sounded disappointed.

The princesses spent the rest of the afternoon working on the contests and lists. When they went down to supper, Annie was still thinking about the contest for honesty. They hadn't been able to come up with anything yet, but she knew how important honesty was to her, and she wanted an honest husband for Snow White.

As they entered the crowded great hall, Annie saw that King Archibald was seated at the head table. The princes had left two seats to one side of the king for Snow White and Annie. Maitland fumed as Annie introduced the four newly arrived princes to Snow White, giving Cozwald an extra-dirty look when the prince walked around the table to kiss Snow White's hand.

"Now let me introduce my other suitors to you," said Snow White as Cozwald returned to his seat. "Prince Milo is from the kingdom of Gulleer to our west."

"I understand that Gulleer's economy is based on shipping," said Liam.

"That's true," said Milo, the corners of his blue eyes crinkling when he smiled. "And we have the largest navy of any kingdom. We would like to expand our interests inland, however," he added, smiling at Snow White.

"And this is Prince Tandry," Snow White said quickly. "He comes from the mountains of Westerling."

"Isn't Westerling full of mystics?" asked Andreas.

"Yes," said Prince Tandry as he traced the grain in the tabletop with his finger. Everyone waited for him to say something else, but he didn't seem to notice.

"And this is Prince Nasheen," Snow White finally said.

"I am from the kingdom of Viramoot," said Nasheen, stroking his mustache with his index finger and thumb. He was older than the other princes, and Annie guessed that he was in his early twenties. "We're known for breeding the finest horses in all the kingdoms. Our bloodstock is second to none."

"I'm not so sure about that," said Andreas. "We breed some excellent horses in Corealis."

Annie sat back to listen while the princes got to know one another, sizing each other up as they debated who had faster horses in their stables or stronger armies in the field or fiercer dragons in their forests. Of the three princes she had never met before, Milo was sitting closest to her. She noticed that after sitting near her for a few minutes, his nose became more prominent, and his ears stuck out to the sides. When she saw that the other princes had noticed as well, she tried not to laugh at the horrified look on Prince Nasheen's face.

Tandry and Nasheen were seated so far from her that any changes in their appearances were too small to notice, but that didn't stop Nasheen from studying all the princes at her end of the table, staring longest at the ones near Annie who had changed the most. She thought that Milo might have noticed the changes in the princes near him; he seemed amused if anything. Annie didn't see any sign that Tandry had noticed, but then he seemed to be in his own world, gazing off into empty air much of the time.

Everyone turned as two serving girls carrying a huge platter between them approached the table. A roasted peacock decorated with its own feathers filled the platter, which took up the entire center of the table when the girls set it down. Everyone at the head table was served as much as they wanted before the platter was carried to the other tables.

The food kept coming after that, and Annie and Liam spent more time eating than talking. Annie had so much she wanted to tell him, but not now in front of all these people. While Snow White listened intently to the princes as they boasted, argued, and tried to impress her, Annie heard only part of the conversation as her thoughts kept wandering back to Snow White's stepmother. Marissa, the evil queen, was on the loose. Although it was possible that Marissa had fled the kingdom, she might well have stayed around, hoping to regain control of the kingdom one way or another. Annie glanced at Liam, certain that he wasn't going to like the news any more than she did.

Annie waited until supper was over and a minstrel was entertaining the diners before touching Liam's arm and whispering into his ear, "We have to talk. Let's go outside."

Pleading a need for fresh air, Annie asked the king for leave. When he granted it with a nod and a wave of his hand, she and Liam slipped from the table. They were on their way out the door when Annie saw Dog begging for scraps. Dog looked at her as if wanting an invitation to join them, but Annie shook her head and motioned for her furry friend to stay.

Once in the courtyard, they looked for a quiet place where they could talk without being overheard. They found such a place between the castle wall and the stable. When Liam pulled her into his arms to kiss her, Annie didn't protest, but after a few minutes she pulled away, saying, "I really did want to come out here to talk."

"I know," he replied with a grin. "But that doesn't mean we can't take care of more important matters first."

Annie caressed his cheek, then shook her head and stepped back a pace. "Snow White told me why she wanted me to come. Her father said that she has to get married right away because he wants her new groom to take her far away. It's for her own protection. Snow White's stepmother escaped from the dungeon, and the king is afraid she might hurt Snow White."

"When did she escape?" asked Liam.

"Only a few days after we left last time," Annie said. "They think she might have had help."

"They're right in thinking that she's dangerous, but I wonder if it's really Snow White she's after."

"Do you think Marissa might be the woman who put that green fire in my hair?" asked Annie. "It never occurred to me that it might be her. I'd thought she was still locked away. I suppose it was possible.... But why would she want to hurt me? If she wants to take over the kingdom again, wouldn't she be more likely to go after Snow White or the king?"

"Not if she wanted to get rid of you first so you couldn't come back to Helmswood to help them."

"Do you think she was the one who sent the crows and followed us all the way back here?" asked Annie.

"I don't know," said Liam. "The message the witch had sent to my mother was signed 'Terobella.' Do you think that might be Marissa's real name?"

"I doubt it. I think it must be someone else entirely. Marissa has lived here for years, but according to Beldegard's mother, Terobella lived in Montrose until recently. You know, when we first heard the name 'Terobella,' I'd thought it sounded vaguely familiar, but I've tried and tried and I can't remember where I might have heard it before."

"Regardless of who the witch really is, you're in danger here, Annie," said Liam. "You have to promise me that you won't do anything foolish or go anywhere alone. I want you to tell me before you do anything out of the ordinary."

"I promise I won't plan to do anything foolish," said Annie, giving his hand a squeeze.

Liam gave her an odd look, as if he was not really satisfied with her answer, but all he said was "Did you tell Snow White about what happened on our way here?"

Annie shook her head. "I thought she already had enough things to worry about."

"I think we should tell her and the king. They need to know what's going on."

"Of course we'll tell them," said Annie, "but I think all it's going to do is make them worry more."

CHAPTER 10

ANNIE LAY AWAKE thinking about Snow White's evil stepmother. If Marissa was in the castle, she would be in disguise. It wouldn't take long to find all the women who had come to the castle only recently and touch them to see who changed. Annie wasn't sure how to go about it without letting Marissa know what she was doing, but she finally decided to get a list of the names and visit each person as casually as possible.

It was easier to go to sleep with a plan in mind. When she woke the next morning, Annie went straight to the steward's office. The man was seated at a table, going over the schedule for the day. When Annie told him what she wanted, he looked at her in surprise.

"I'm sorry, Your Highness, but you and Princess Snow White are the only ladies to have arrived at the castle recently. When Queen Marissa was here, many people left. Even more left when she escaped from the dungeon, fearing what she would do in reprisal. I can give you a list of the women who live here, but that's the best I can do."

Annie thought for a moment. If so many people had fled the castle, couldn't Marissa have returned and taken on the appearance of one of the woman who had actually gone? If the real woman left because she was afraid, she might not have told anyone that she was leaving, so no one would think it odd that she was still here. Finding Marissa was going to take a lot longer than she'd first thought, and it looked as if Annie was going to have to touch every woman in the castle.

"That list will be fine," Annie told the steward. "I'm going to need the names of the ladies of the court, as well as all the women who work here. And please be thorough. What I have planned won't work unless I have every single name."

"Very good, Your Highness. I'll have them ready as soon as I can."

Annie sighed as she left the steward's office. What had seemed like a simple task was suddenly becoming much more complicated.

~

Liam had volunteered to speak to the king that morning to tell him what had happened on their way to Helmswood. When Annie went to the small dining room where the family ate, Liam, Snow White, and four of the princes were there eating fruit, cheese, and boiled eggs.

"Did you meet with the king yet?" Annie asked, taking the chair next to Liam's.

"Indeed, I did," said Liam. "He was very concerned and apologetic because he's convinced that his wife was the one who put the flowers in your hair. He says he's going to hire more guards to watch for her. And there's something else. A messenger arrived from my father last night. He sent a patrol to check on Granny Bentbone, but the tower was empty when they arrived."

Annie was horrified, and it must have shown on her face because Liam placed his hand on her arm and gave it a comforting squeeze. "How did Granny Bentbone get out?" she asked.

Liam shrugged. "The men didn't see anything she could have used. My guess is it was either magic or someone helped her."

"We have to find her again!" said Annie. "She's too dangerous to remain on the loose."

"My father already sent word to your father. By now they probably both have men out looking for her. There's nothing we could do that they won't be doing already."

"I suppose," said Annie, "but I feel responsible. We were the ones who suggested the tower."

"Actually, it was my idea and I wasn't even sure if it was a good one. I'm sorry, Annie. It's my fault, not yours."

"We'll just have to hope they find her soon," said Annie. "Otherwise we'll go help when we're finished here. So, what did Snow White's father say when you told him about Terobella's letter and the crows?"

Liam reached for a peach and eyed it while he said, "Just that he's never heard of her, but he'll have his guards watch for her, too."

"Father told me about what happened to you on the way here," said Snow White. "How dreadful for you!"

Digby looked up from selecting another boiled egg. "Are you talking about what happened in the marsh? Nasty business. We were lucky I got away with my life."

"We wouldn't have let anything happen to you," Emilio said, shaking his head. "But you shouldn't have gone off the path in the first place."

"I was the only one looking for a way out!" exclaimed Digby.

"When you've finished eating, could I speak with you alone?" Annie asked Snow White.

"Of course! Is something else wrong?" Snow White asked, her eyes growing wide.

"No, no! It's nothing like that. I just need you to help me with something, if you wouldn't mind."

"I'd be happy to help, but it can't take too long. I told Father about the contest and he's going to call a meeting with all the princes at noon. He wants me to announce the contest then."

"What contest?" asked Maitland.

"There will be tests of skill, I am sure," said Nasheen. "I myself am an excellent rider."

"You'll learn all about it at noon today," said Snow White. "Annie, we should probably go now if you want my help. Noon will be here before we know it."

Liam gave Annie a quizzical look as she snatched some fruit and followed Snow White out of the room. She'd thought about telling him what she had planned, but the way he was acting lately, he'd probably try to stop her. And while she had promised not to plan anything foolish, this wasn't foolish and it was going to work!

"Now, what is this all about?" Snow White asked once they'd reached the privacy of her chamber.

"I believe I can find your stepmother if she is in the castle, but I need your help to do it," said Annie.

"I'll do anything if it will find Marissa. What do you want me to do? Help yc locate all the secret passages so we can spy through peepholes? I know of two passages behind the walls, but I'm sure there are more."

Annie shook her head. "Nothing like that. I just want you to introduce me to the noblewomen in the castle. I think Marissa is probably here posing as someone we wouldn't ordinarily suspect. She might even have taken the place of someone you know, so I need to meet all of them." When Snow White looked baffled, Annie said, "Magic doesn't work around me, remember? If I touch her, the magic she's using to disguise herself will disappear, and we'll see what she really looks like."

"Oh, I'm sure that's a very good idea," said Snow White. "It's just that it sounds really tiresome. I thought you had something exciting in mind."

Annie bit her lip, holding back what she really wanted to say. Why was Snow White taking her plan so casually? Not exciting enough! Annie was there to help her, not entertain her! "Sorry, it's the best I can do," she finally said. "Will you help me?"

Snow White stood and straightened her gown. "We'll start right now. Let's see who we run into first. I suppose it's a good thing so many people left the castle when Marissa was in control. There are far fewer people here now than when I was a little girl."

They had scarcely started down the corridor when Snow White called, "Lady Polette! I'd like you to meet someone."

A noblewoman who had been walking in the other direction stopped and turned around. "Yes, Your Highness?" she said, looking surprised.

"This is my friend Princess Annabelle of Treecrest. I don't believe you've met."

Lady Polette curtsied, saying, "No, Your Highness. I don't believe we have."

Annie couldn't think of any reason to touch her, until she noticed that the woman was wearing gaudy jewelry. "What an interesting ring," she said. "May I see it?"

Lady Polette looked flustered, as if she thought Annie wanted the ring for herself. When the noblewoman began to pull it from her finger, Annie said, "Oh, no. You don't have to take it off," and reached for her hand. Annie touched her long enough to admire the ring and wait for any magic the woman had to fade away. Without the magic that made her attractive, Lady Polette had a long, narrow face that reminded Annie of a horse, but she didn't look anything like Snow White's stepmother.

"It was lovely meeting you," Annie said, releasing the noblewoman's hand.

Lady Polette curtsied again as Annie and Snow White walked away. "We're going to have to think of a reason for me to touch them," said Annie. "Maybe I could hand them something."

"You could give them a handkerchief if they have a runny nose," suggested Snow White.

Annie laughed and shook her head. "I don't have that many handkerchiefs, and I doubt very many noblewomen will have runny noses."

"I know!" said Snow White. "We'll get one of the gardeners to pick some flowers for us. You can hand each lady a single blossom!"

"That would work," said Annie.

"We'll go to the garden now. You can bump into women on the way!"

"That will make a good first impression!" Annie said, laughing again.

They met three more noblewomen on the way to the garden, and Annie managed to bump into each one. After meeting them, Annie made a point of memorizing their names so she could tick them off her list.

The steward had also made up a list of all the women who worked in the castle. Annie was about to call to a maid, but the girl scurried away when she saw the two princesses. "I need to talk to all the women," said Annie, "including the servants."

"That's not going to be easy," said Snow White. "They've been awfully skittish since my stepmother escaped."

"I'm sure I'll think of something," Annie said, though she wasn't sure at all.

The head gardener ran to meet them when they entered the garden. Annie admired the roses while Snow White told the man to pick all the flowers that would fit in a basket and bring the basket to Princess Annabelle after the meeting with the princes. As soon as he was dismissed, the man ran about, giving orders to his helpers.

"It must be close to noon," Snow White said, glancing at the position of the sun. "We should go to the meeting now. I'll help you more later if I have time."

"This is going to take forever," said Annie. "I can use all the help I can get!"

The princesses made their way to the king's audience chamber, where the princes were already waiting. Snow White stayed with Annie until King Archibald came in, then went to sit beside him.

"I've decided how I will choose the prince that I will marry," Snow White announced. "There will be trials, but not of the usual sort. No one will be sent on a quest. Instead, each of you must determine how you will prove your worth to me. The trials will start in the morning. In the first trial, you will have to express how you feel about me in a creative way. It is up to you to decide how you will do this."

"What?" said Digby. "We have to decide what we're going to do? I've never heard of such a thing."

Nasheen looked indignant. "This is quite irregular. Princes never have to think for themselves in situations like this."

"I'm not sure what to do," called Milo. "Tell us what you want."

"I already told you enough," said Snow White. "The rest is up to you." The king leaned toward her and whispered something in her ear. Snow White nodded and stood. "If you'll excuse me, I'll see you tomorrow. You will have until tomorrow's supper to complete your task."

When Snow White and her father left the room, the

princes turned to Annie. "You must know what she wants," said Emilio. "Can't you give us some ideas?"

Annie shook her head. "It's Snow White's contest. It was up to her to tell you what she thought you needed to know. Good day, gentlemen, and good luck!"

Annie hurried from the room, unhappy that Snow White had left her there without warning to face the princes by herself. She could understand why they were confused; even she had expected her friend to give the suitors at least some sort of example. But there was nothing she could do about it now.

The head gardener was waiting when she entered the corridor, ready with a basket full of flowers. She smiled and thanked him, then glanced down at the basket with dismay. Without Snow White to help, she had no idea how she was ever going to find all these women. She supposed that she'd have to find Snow White first.

Although Annie knew where her friend's chamber was located, the way was confusing and it took her a while to find it. When no one answered Annie's knock, she finally admitted that she'd have to do without Snow White's help. Annoyed, Annie began to approach the women by herself. It was awkward without Snow White there to introduce her, especially when Annie had to ask the women their names. She would have to cross them off her list back in her room.

Annie spent the rest of the afternoon wandering

through the castle, handing out flowers to the ladies of the court. Each time she met one, she noted what happened when she touched the lady's hand. Every once in a while she'd return to her room to check off names and see how many she had left. The number was dwindling, but she didn't feel she was getting anywhere.

The shadows were growing long when she handed out the last blossom in the basket. She was wondering how much the ladies of the court appreciated the small gift when Lady Chantry dropped the flower as she walked away. "Did she do that on purpose because she doesn't want it, or was that an accident?" Annie murmured to herself. She was trying to decide if she should call out to the noblewoman when a courtier scooped the flower off the floor and dashed after Lady Chantry. As he handed the flower back to the lady, Annie had an idea. She knew exactly what the honesty test would be, but it wasn't going to involve flowers.

Annie went to supper that night planning to ask her friend where she'd been, but neither Snow White nor the king was there. Tired and in a foul mood, Annie knew that she wouldn't make very good company, so she asked to have some food brought to her chamber. She was about to leave when Maitland spotted her.

"I need to talk to you," he said, cornering her outside the hall. "You have to give me some idea of what she wants. I already can't sleep for thinking of her. I was a fool for talking about her to my friends when I first met her. Now I need to show her how much she means to me. Please, Annie, what does she want from us?"

"I really can't say …," Annie began.

"I'm not asking you to tell me what to do, just what she meant when she said that we have to express how we feel about her."

Annie sighed, knowing that she wasn't going to get away without telling him something. "I'll tell you this much, but you have to tell the other princes as well. Think of what you know about Snow White and what you think might please her. Think about your own talents and create something she would like that would mean something to her. I really can't tell you more than that. Now, good night, Maitland. I wish you well in whatever you decide to do."

CHAPTER 11

LIAM MET ANNIE in the corridor outside her room the next morning. "I missed you at supper last night," he said.

"I'm sorry," said Annie. "But I just couldn't face the princes again. I don't have any better idea what to tell them now than I did last night. I can't believe Snow White didn't tell them more. And she was supposed to help me with something, but she never showed up. Don't you think that when you're helping someone, she should do what she can to help you help her?"

"Uh…," said Liam.

"I mean," continued Annie, "I wasn't wandering around the castle with a basket of flowers for fun! I am sorry that I didn't send word to you that I wouldn't be at supper, though."

"That's all right, but I must admit, without you to talk to, supper was tedious. If the princes weren't boasting about how great their creations are going to be, they were worried that they aren't doing what Snow White wants. When I stopped by the small dining room this morning, they were still talking about what they were going to do. I didn't think you wanted to hear it, so I picked this up in the kitchen," he said, handing her a soft folded cloth.

"You were right," Annie said, smiling up at him. "Thank you for thinking of this!" She unfolded the cloth, revealing oatcakes plump with currants. "This is perfect. I was wondering how I was going to get through the morning without breakfast."

"I understand that there's a well with exceptionally tasty water near the north gate." Liam smiled and hooked her arm through his. "I thought we could walk while we eat and quench our thirst at the well. There are guards on the walls, and I've come armed, so the crows shouldn't bother us," he said, patting the sword at his side.

"That sounds like a marvelous plan," said Annie. "I'd enjoy seeing something other than the inside of this castle."

"I know a shortcut," Liam told her as he led her to a stairwell she hadn't seen before. "I make a point of exploring every castle we visit whenever possible. You never know when being able to find your way around the less public places might come in handy."

"Like when we want to avoid lovesick princes?" said Annie as they started down the stairs.

"Precisely," said Liam. "Or when we want to leave in a hurry, or find something the owners don't want us to find."

"Or invade it someday," said Annie.

"Uh-huh, or listen in on secrets."

"Or learn where everything is so you won't get lost when you sleepwalk and wake to find yourself in a strange corridor?"

"I hadn't thought of that one!" said Liam. "Although I might have if I actually walked in my sleep. Ah, here we are. I believe that's the door we want straight ahead."

It was a beautiful day when they stepped outside. Annie tilted her head to let the sunshine warm her face. Castles were usually chilly inside, and it was nice to feel warm for a change. She glanced down when she heard Dog bark, "Hello! What are you doing here?"

"Going for a walk," said Annie. "Would you like to go with us?"

"Would I!" Dog said, wagging her tail. "I love walks! Where are we going?"

"To the well by the north gate," Liam told her.

"Really! Really!" Dog shouted, so excited that her whole body wiggled. "I love water! Follow me!"

Annie laughed when Dog ran ahead, disappearing around a corner.

"Look," said Liam. "There are carvings on the wall. Is that a dragon?"

"I think so. And see there! That's a gargoyle on the roof."

"And a crow," Liam said, frowning.

Annie raised her hand to shade her eyes from the sun and looked farther down the roof to where a crow sat atop one of the gargoyles. Tilting its head, it eyed Annie before flying off.

"There are more over there," said Liam, nodding toward the wall, where a small flock had gathered.

"If only crows didn't all look alike. There's no way to tell if they're the ones that were following us or not," Annie said, and took a bite of an oatcake.

A scullery maid dressed in a cape made from ratty scraps of fur walked past carrying full buckets in either hand. She was humming and looked cheerful until she chanced to see Annie and Liam. Freezing like a deer in firelight, she suddenly bolted, disappearing between two buildings.

"I didn't know we were that scary," Liam said with a frown.

"I don't think it's us. Or at least I hope not," said Annie. "I think that—"

There was a cracking sound overhead, and Liam looked up.

"Annie, look out!" he shouted, knocking her to the side as part of a gargoyle tumbled from the roof and hit the ground right where she had been standing.

Annie lay sprawled on the hard-packed dirt, her

breath knocked out of her. Struggling to sit up, she looked for Liam in the plume of dust that the gargoyle had kicked up when it hit. As the dust settled, Liam was already getting back on his feet. He reached for her hand, and she noticed a streak of blood on his cheek.

"You're bleeding!" cried Annie.

Liam touched his cheek with his other hand even as he pulled her up. "It's just a scratch."

"Ho!" shouted a guard from the top of the wall. "Is anyone hurt?"

"No," Liam called back. "Did you see what happened?"

"I saw the whole thing," shouted the guard. "There was no one there, then suddenly that gargoyle broke in half and fell. If you hadn't pushed the girl, she would have been killed."

"If no one was there . . . ," said Annie.

"It had to be either magic or a crow for it to fall in that precise spot. Perhaps coming outside wasn't such a good idea," Liam said, looking up at the roof.

Dog came trotting over to sniff the gargoyle. When she noticed the oatcakes that Annie had dropped, she devoured them one after another without stopping to breathe in between. When she was finished, she licked her lips and turned to Annie. "Why would someone leave perfectly good food like that lying on the ground?"

"I just dropped them," Annie told her.

"Oh, did you want them?"

"No!" Annie laughed. "Not after they were covered with dirt."

"I don't understand humans," said Dog. "Food is food, no matter where you find it. I need some water now. That food made me thirsty. I know! I'll go to the well by the north gate!"

As Dog disappeared again, Liam took Annie's arm and steered her to the door. "I'm sorry I suggested that we come out here!"

"I'm glad you did," Annie said as the door closed behind them. "We both needed the fresh air and sunshine, but now I think the air inside might prove to be healthier."

"Listen to me!" Liam said, turning her so she faced him. "I don't want you going outside, not while the witch is still around! You can live without fresh air and sunshine for a while. Stay inside. You're safer here. Tell me, what do you plan to do now?"

"I was going to ask the gardener for some more flowers, although I suppose I could send someone to ask him for me. First, I'm going back to my room to clean up. I seem to be wearing a layer of dust." She patted her arm to show him, and the dust that rose made them both sneeze.

"Good idea," said Liam. "I should probably do the same, but first I'm going to talk to Captain Sterling and see what we can do to help King Archibald strengthen his guard. If you want to go anywhere, send for me.

I don't want you walking around here alone and unprotected."

They said good-bye at Annie's door. After giving him a kiss, she watched him walk down the corridor. She was sure a witch had made the gargoyle fall, but which woman could it be? Queen Marissa might well be here, but the crows were probably Terobella's. After all, it was Terobella who had sent the note to Liam's mother promising that her crows would help Queen Lenore if she killed Annie. Annie assumed that meant the crows were Terobella's. But did that mean that she was here as well? Could the two witches be working together? And why would they want to? Was she getting close to finding one of them? Or maybe one of the witches had something in mind and wanted Annie out of the way.

She was just opening her door when Horace appeared. "Your Highness, is everything all right?"

"Yes, of course," she replied. "Why do you ask?"

"My nephew Niko saw a falling gargoyle come close to hitting you," he said. "I just wanted to make sure that you weren't hurt. Your father would never forgive me if something happened to you when I was supposed to be keeping watch."

"No need to worry, Horace. I wasn't injured. So you have family here?"

"Oh yes," said Horace. "Niko and his wife, Marta, and her sister Tesia all work in the castle. I've been visiting Niko and his wife in the evening when they get off work."

"Really?" said Annie. "Then perhaps you can help me."

Horace's eyes lit up. "Whatever you need, Your Highness. How may I be of service?"

Annie glanced up and down the corridor. She didn't see anyone, but it was better not to take chances. She gestured him into her room, then waited until she'd shut the door before saying, "Snow White's stepmother is a witch and can use magic to change her appearance. We think she's in the castle disguised as someone else."

"Niko and Marta told me all about Queen Marissa, and none of it was good. There's a lot of fear in this castle, and it's all because of her."

"Maybe I can do something about that. I'm trying to locate the queen by coming into contact with every woman in the castle. I hope to touch her and show what she really looks like."

Horace nodded. "I can see how that would work. But she's an evil woman, so you'll need protection when you find her. I'll stand by your side just in case."

"That's a good idea," said Annie. She hadn't really thought about what would happen when she located the witch other than that the woman couldn't cast a spell on her. She hadn't even told Liam what she was doing, something she probably should have done at the very beginning. Now that she thought about it, she decided that it probably would be a good idea to have someone armed nearby. Even if Annie could negate the witch's magic, Marissa might be dangerous in other ways.

"There's something else I need you to do for me," she told Horace. "I want to talk to the women who work in the castle as well as the women of noble birth. Could you and your relatives bring the women who work here to me one at a time so I can make sure they are who they say they are?"

"We should be able to manage that!" said Horace. "Should I bring them to your chamber?"

"No, we'll find an empty room somewhere else. I don't want Snow White's stepmother to know what we're doing until we've found her, if she doesn't already know, that is," Annie said, thinking of the falling gargoyle. "I know! We'll tell the women that we're looking for ideas to surprise the princes. Then they won't be able to tell anyone what we're really doing."

"I think I can get Marta and Tesia to help, but I might have to tell them the truth. They hated the queen and will do whatever it takes to make sure she leaves for good. They're honest women and can keep a secret if we ask them."

"If you really think it will help and that they won't tell anyone," said Annie.

"I'm sure of it. Why don't I go locate a room while you freshen up. You have a bit of a smudge here," Horace said, rubbing his cheekbone. "And your hair—well, I'm sure you know what I mean."

"Yes, thank you, Horace," Annie said, knowing that she must be a real mess if Horace felt the need to point it out. "I'll wait for you here. Come get me when you've found a room we can use."

Liam had insisted that she send for him, but she didn't think he'd mind if she took Horace instead. All Liam had wanted was that she have someone with her. If Horace's relatives could help, her task would be that much easier.

As soon as she shut the door, Annie checked her reflection in the mirror. She had dirt on her face and a piece of hay tangled in her hair. Her clothes were rumpled and dusty, and she had a great dirty patch on one side of her gown. "Mother would have a fit if she saw me like this," she murmured, pulling the hay from her hair.

Annie didn't have time to send for water to fill a tub, so she used the washbowl that the maids kept filled, even though the water was cold. After washing her face and hands, she brushed her hair until it shone. Hearing that Annie had lost many of her things in the carriage accident, Snow White had given her some of the new gowns that the castle seamstresses had made for her. Although Annie was a little smaller than Snow White, the gowns fit fairly well.

Annie had just pulled on a soft blue gown when

there was a knock on her door. "Just a minute!" she called, thinking it was Horace.

"It's me, Snow White!"

When Annie opened the door, Snow White hurried into the room and perched on a chair by the window.

"Where were you yesterday?" Annie asked her. "I thought you were going to help me."

"Was I?" said Snow White. "I spent the entire afternoon with my father. We had so much to talk about, although he did most of the talking. He loved my mother very much and never intended to marry again until he met Marissa. He didn't intend to marry her, either, but he thinks she must have used magic on him. I don't know how many times he told me that he was a fool for marrying her and that she was a terrible wife even when she wasn't drugging him."

"I believe him," said Annie.

Snow White was wearing her long black hair loose down her back. She picked up a lock of hair that was draped across her shoulder and began to inspect it. "We talked about Maitland, too," she said. "Father likes him, but then he wasn't the one who overheard Maitland talking to his friends. Do you know what I wish?" Snow White said, dropping the lock of hair and turning to Annie. "I wish Maitland had never come here! I get so confused when he's around."

"Then you must have some sort of feelings for him," said Annie. "If you truly hated him, you wouldn't be confused."

"But I really can't stand him! He said some awful things, and I don't want to have anything to do with him."

"He's here as one of your suitors, and you didn't tell him that he couldn't compete in the contest," Annie said.

"I know," said Snow White. "And I don't know what to do. I probably should have told him to go away when he got here, but I just couldn't. It wouldn't have been fair to turn him back after he traveled all the way here, and one thing I'm determined to be is fair. So many things aren't fair, you know, but if you complain about it, people always say, 'Life isn't fair!' Well, it should be! And now Maitland is here and in the contest, and I don't want to talk to him even though he keeps sending me flowers and notes and asking to see me."

"I don't know what he said to make you so upset, but I do know that he's sorry he said it," Annie told her.

"Then he shouldn't have said it in the first place!" cried Snow White.

"Haven't you ever said something that you later regretted?" Annie asked. "Something that you would take back if you could, but you can't and it makes you miserable?"

"I suppose," said Snow White. "Although I never said

anything half as bad! Honestly, this whole thing makes my head hurt. I wish I could go home!"

"But you are home," said Annie.

"I mean the cottage in the forest. It's the only place where I was truly happy. I miss the cottage, and I miss the seven dwarves. They were like the brothers I never had."

Both princesses turned around when there was a knock on the door. "That's probably Horace," said Annie. "He was taking care of something for me."

"I need to leave now anyway," said Snow White as she got to her feet. "I promised Father that I'd walk with him in the garden."

Snow White nodded at Horace as she left the room. "I'll be right with you," Annie told him while she gathered her list, a quill, and a pot of ink.

"I've found a room we can use," Horace said when Annie finally joined him. "Marta and Tesia are going to help. They'll bring the women to us one at a time."

"You're very efficient," Annie said, closing the door behind her.

"When I told them what you were doing, they got excited. They promised not to tell anyone, but they can't wait to get rid of Marissa once and for all."

"I'm glad they're glad," Annie told him. "I was worried that they might be so afraid of the queen that they wouldn't want to talk to me in case she found out. I was even worried that someone who lived here might have been the one to help Marissa get free."

Horace shook his head. "That would never have happened. No one wants her loose in the castle ever again."

≈

The room Horace had found was in the same corridor as the steward's office. It was a small room with a large table, a few chairs, and a single window facing the guards' barracks. When Annie walked in, two plump, middle-aged women turned from the window and curtsied so low that Annie was afraid they'd fall over.

"Your Highness, I'd like you to meet my nephew's wife, Marta, and her sister, Tesia," said Horace. "Marta, you can fetch the first woman."

"If it pleases Your Highness, I thought I would be first," said Marta.

"And so you should be, Marta. Thank you so much for helping us with this. May I touch your hand?" asked Annie.

"What? Oh, why, yes. That's how you do it, then. I wasn't sure," Marta said, extending her hand to Annie. "How long will this take?"

"No time at all," said Annie, releasing the woman. No magic had been used to change Marta, so Annie's touch had no effect on her.

"That was it?" Marta asked, looking confused.

"That was it!" Annie smiled and turned to Marta's sister. "Tesia?"

When nothing changed about Tesia, either, Horace shooed the two women out the door, sending them to fetch others. Annie spent the rest of the day seeing one woman after another. By the time the shadow of the barracks blocked the sun from the window, she had seen over half the women on her list, and it was time for her to get dressed for supper.

"I never did see the scullery maid wearing the fur," said Annie, scanning her list.

"A scullery maid in furs?" said Horace. "Now, where would a girl like that get the money for such things?"

"Not nice furs like the nobles wear, but little scraps like rat or mice or squirrel all sewn together. Liam and I saw her when we were outside today."

"I'll ask Marta," Horace told her. "We'll get her to bring the girl tomorrow."

CHAPTER 12

ANNIE TOOK THE LIST BACK to her room and tucked it away under some clothes in a trunk. It took her only a few minutes to change her gown and start for the stairs. She was surprised to find Snow White waiting for her outside the great hall.

"There you are!" said Snow White. "I wondered why I didn't see you today. What have you been up to?"

"Checking people off my list," Annie whispered back. "Do you have a moment to talk before we go in?"

"Yes, but just a moment. The princes are going to give me their gifts tonight, and I don't want to be late."

Annie pulled Snow White down the corridor so they were out of the way of the people entering the hall. "I thought of what we can do for the honesty test."

"Is that all?" said Snow White. "I thought you might have found Marissa. Oh well, don't give up. I'm sure you'll find her sooner or later."

"Yes, but the test for honesty…"

"Whatever you decide will be fine. We don't have time to go into that now. Just let me know who passed the test when you're finished. We should go to our seats. Father will be here any minute, and I'm dying to see what the princes brought me!"

Annie followed Snow White into the great hall, annoyed that her friend couldn't be bothered to listen to her plan. Even if Snow White didn't care, she could pretend to be interested, at least!

"Father!" Snow White said when they had taken their seats and the king finally appeared. "Will we eat first or see what the princes have done?"

King Archibald chuckled. "We'll eat, of course! A little more suspense will only make the food taste better! Don't you agree?" he said, turning to the princes seated across from him.

The princes nodded like a group of dolls, and a few smiled brightly at Snow White. Maitland looked miserable, as if he was sure he was going to lose, while Tandry seemed calm, his face a serene mask that betrayed little of what he was thinking. Most of the others fiddled with their tankards or tore pieces of bread into little bits. Although Nasheen seemed relaxed and confident, he frowned when he looked at Annie. Something told her that he had learned why the princes who sat near her changed.

Liam chuckled when Milo reached for another

piece of bread to crumble. "I'm sure they wish this evening were over," he whispered to Annie. "I can't wait to see what you girls have come up with for the next test. What superior trait are they supposed to show tomorrow?"

"Two, actually. Bravery and honesty," Annie told him, giggling when she saw how frightened Milo looked. "I think some of them could use a little bravery right now."

Although the roasted venison, goose, and trout were delicious and plentiful, the princes ate very little, picking at the food they took and turning most away. Only Nasheen, Liam, the king, and the two princesses seemed to have any appetite. When a servant carried off the last platter, the princes became even more nervous.

"Now, then," said Snow White. "Who would like to go first?"

"I should," said Digby, "because mine is part of supper. Girl!" he called, waving to a serving girl carrying a large platter. "You may serve it now."

The girl hurried forward to set a small iced cake in front of each person at the table. Piled high with icing, the confection looked like snow mounded on a rooftop and sparkled with sugar crystals.

Snow White was the first to taste it. "Did you make this yourself?" she asked. "It's delicious!"

"Me, slaving away in a kitchen?" said Digby. "Not

likely! But I did find out what your favorite dessert is and told your cooks how to change it with a few ideas of my own. I call it Frosted Snow, in your honor, my lady."

"How thoughtful," Snow White told him with a smile. "Now, who would like to be next?"

"I would," said Cozwald, getting to his feet. "I have written a poem to express my love and admiration." Taking a piece of parchment from his pocket, he held it up and read:

> *Hair as black as night,*
> *Skin as white as snow,*
> *Lips as red as blood,*
> *Makes my own heart glow.*
>
> *Beauty so unique*
> *Is a real treasure.*
> *If I made you mine,*
> *I'd love you beyond measure.*

"What did you think of it?" Snow White whispered to Annie. "You've spent your whole life at court and know more about these things."

"The last line was a little off," Annie began.

"The whole thing was a little off, if you ask me," Liam said, smiling behind his hand.

"I'd like to go next," said Emilio. Nodding to two

musicians waiting behind the table, he bowed to Snow White, saying, "I have prepared a dance that I thought would best express my feelings."

"You've got to be joking," Liam whispered to Annie.

Nasheen snorted when Emilio struck a pose. The instant the musicians started to play, Emilio began to twirl. His dancing was choppy at first, but it soon became more fluid. Annie thought he was good at expressing some emotions, like longing, fear, and joy, but she didn't understand most of it and got a little confused when he jumped into the air and almost landed on another table.

"That was very energetic," Annie whispered when Snow White leaned close.

"I rather liked it," Snow White told her. "It reminds me of the way I danced when I was alone in the woods."

"Which is exactly how a dance like that should be performed," whispered Liam. "Alone. And in the woods."

"I made you something, Princess," Milo said, gesturing to someone in the shadows. A man came forward carrying something covered with a cloth and set it on the table in front of the prince. Milo whipped the cloth off with a flourish, uncovering a twisted, knotted rope worked into the shape of a face. "See, I used knots to make a portrait of you. Those are your eyes and this is your nose." He pointed to each of the features as he spoke. "I unraveled some rope for your hair."

"I can see that," said Snow White. "It's quite inventive."

"Pictures like this are a treasured art form in my kingdom," Milo told her. "Everyone in Gulleer learns how to tie knots at an early age."

"I've never seen anything like it," Annie told Snow White.

"And you probably never will again," said Digby. "Imagine, giving a princess a pile of rope!"

Milo scowled at him, but he looked more cheerful when Snow White gave him an encouraging smile. "And who will be next?" she asked, turning to the other princes.

"Perhaps some more music is in order," said Andreas. "I've prepared a song and will accompany myself on my lute."

"I didn't know Andreas could play," Cozwald said.

"Shh!" said his cousin. "I want to hear this!"

Strumming the first few notes, Andreas began to sing:

I held a contest to find my bride,
But I was led astray.
I kissed a beauty sound asleep,
But she loved someone else.
I traveled far to reach your side,
Though danger tried to stop me.
And when I saw you the first time,

I knew we were meant to be.
Oh yes—We were meant to be!
Oh, we were meant to be!

"That song is meant to be over," declared Digby.

"He has a nice voice," Annie told Snow White.

"The best thing you can say about his lute playing," said Cozwald, "is that someone used some very nice wood to make the instrument."

"You're being awfully quiet, Maitland. Are you all right?" Annie asked him.

Maitland nodded and reached for something under his seat. "Yes, of course. I was just enjoying the entertainment. Here, Princess, I made this for you." He handed Snow White a large piece of parchment and sat back to watch her face.

Annie leaned toward Snow White for a closer look. "Oh!" she said when she saw what her friend was holding. It was a drawing done in ink of Snow White and the seven dwarves in front of the little cottage in the woods. Although Maitland had to have done it from memory, every detail was accurate, from the features on the dwarves' faces to the flowers nodding beside the front door.

"That's beautiful," said Annie. "And you all look so happy!"

"It's very good," Snow White said with a catch in her voice.

"What is that place?" asked Nasheen. "It looks like a woodcutter's cottage."

"It's my home," Snow White replied, rubbing her eyes with the back of her hand. Rather than smiling when she glanced at Maitland, she gave him a look that showed a truer emotion than she had all evening. It was a look of yearning so strong that Annie felt tears come to her own eyes. "It's where I spent the happiest days of my life," Snow White added. "I didn't know anyone knew how much I loved it, but this says it quite clearly. I miss the cottage and the dwarves so much! Thank you, Maitland."

Maitland didn't say anything, but they shared a look that made Liam clear his throat and Nasheen scowl.

"I would like to share my gift with you, but it is outside, so I think I should go last," said Nasheen.

"I wanted to go last," said Tandry. He looked petulant for a moment, but when he saw everyone looking at him, his expression became serene once again. "But I will be next if you would like, Princess. I, too, have a poem for you." He opened a piece of parchment and read in a clear voice,

A pretty girl is like a flower
That blooms in the summer.
She stands alone
In a garden of weeds.

"Uh...," said Snow White, for once at a loss for words. She gave Tandry a halfhearted smile.

"At least it was short," said Digby.

Annie didn't like it, certain that Tandry probably considered her one of the weeds. Liam must have seen her expression because he reached for her hand and squeezed it under the table.

"Thank you," Snow White finally said to Tandry. "Now," she said, turning to Nasheen, "why don't you show us what you've done?"

"It would be my pleasure," said the prince as he rose to his feet. "Please, follow me."

Liam still held Annie's hand when they walked outside. "Do you have any idea where he's taking us?" she asked as they descended the steps into the courtyard.

"I think I do," he said. "Nasheen spent all day loitering in the great hall. I never saw him actually work on anything, so I have my suspicions, especially if we turn left and ... yes! We're going to the stables."

"Here she is!" Nasheen said as a groom led a horse out of the shadows. "I chose this beauty for you out of my own stables, Princess. I was going to present her to you when we announced our engagement, but I believe that she expresses perfectly how I feel about you, so I am giving her to you now. I have renamed her Purity in your honor, for she is as fair and pure in her way as you are in yours."

Annie loved horses and had to admit that the mare

was beautiful, with her creamy coat and flowing mane and tail. But Nasheen hadn't put much effort into the test if all he had done was rename a horse he'd already intended to give to Snow White.

"She's lovely," said Snow White. "But I haven't ridden a horse in eight years. I'm not sure we're well suited for each other."

"Nonsense!" declared Nasheen. "I myself will instruct you in riding! See, I am giving you the best gift, a horse and the exhilaration that you will feel when you race the wind on her back for the first time!"

"That is a very nice gift, Nasheen," Snow White said. "Thank you all for everything you did," she continued, turning to speak to all of the princes. "I will announce your next test tomorrow morning. Be in the small dining hall by eight o'clock. Good night, everyone. Sleep well."

"Bravery, huh?" Liam said to Annie as they drifted back inside. "That should be interesting."

"I know," Annie replied as he put his arm around her shoulder. "Especially with this group of princes."

Chapter 13

Annie woke early the next morning. She had decided during the night that she needed to talk to Liam before Snow White announced the princes' tasks for the day, so she hurried to his room as soon as she had washed and dressed. He had already left his room, however, so she ran down the stairs, still hoping to catch him before he took his seat in the small dining hall. She found him in the corridor outside the hall, talking to Maitland and Andreas. As she approached, Nasheen came out of the room and saw the three princes talking.

"I hope you are not helping these gentlemen," Nasheen said to Liam. "I understand that they are friends of yours, but such assistance would be unfair, and the rest of us would not take it kindly."

"We weren't discussing the contest, if that's what you mean," said Liam.

"Actually, we were talking about the increased

number of crows outside the castle," Maitland told Nasheen. "We think we're going to get some archery practice in later today."

Andreas nodded. "You may join us if you'd like. We could always use another strong arm good with a bow."

"Is this a private competition, or do you really hate crows so much?" asked Nasheen.

"We don't have anything against crows in general, just these particular crows. As for a competition, it may end up becoming one. You never can tell," Andreas said with a grin.

"Liam, may I have a word with you?" Annie asked him.

Liam turned and greeted her with a smile. "Good morning! What would you like to discuss?" he asked as he and Annie drifted farther down the corridor.

"In a little while, Snow White is going to announce the princes' task for today. When the princes leave the room, I'd like to have a guard follow each one, but they need to be discreet. I don't want the princes to know that they're being followed. Although I'm sure the princes are men of great integrity, it wouldn't hurt to have someone keep an eye on them to tell us what each one actually did. I've often found that events tend to get exaggerated when men talk of their bravery. I don't want the guards to interfere with what the princes do, but I suppose they could step in if the young men get into trouble."

Liam nodded. "That's an excellent suggestion. I'll speak with Captain Sterling right away."

"I didn't mean for you to miss breakfast," said Annie.

"This shouldn't take long. I'm sure I'll be back before everyone finishes eating." Giving her a quick kiss on her cheek, Liam strode off down the corridor past the men filing into the dining hall.

Annie took her regular seat beside Snow White, making sure that Liam's chair, on her other side, remained empty.

Milo sat down across from her. "I don't suppose you could give us a clue about what we're supposed to do today?" he said, sounding hopeful. Annie liked Milo, although she wasn't sure he was right for Snow White. He looked and acted younger than the other princes, and the only things he seemed to take seriously were ships and sailing.

Annie looked up as Snow White entered the room on her father's arm. "Snow White is here now," she told the prince. "She'll tell you what you need to know."

"I was just wondering if we'd be going outside," Milo said, glancing toward one of the windows. "It's a beautiful day, with enough wind to fill some sails, if there were any real ships around here."

When Snow White reached her place at the table, she remained standing while her father sat down. "Good morning, everyone," she said. "Today's test is for bravery. You are to find a way to prove that you are brave and come back to tell me about it at supper. Good luck, and I'll see you tonight."

"I will need someone to fight," said Nasheen. "I have proven my bravery many times in combat."

"I'm my best at tournaments," said Cozwald. "You should have seen me at the tournament last spring, Princess!"

"Are there any trolls around that I can chase off?" asked Andreas. "I've never actually seen a troll, but I've always wanted to give it a try."

"I suppose I can look for dragons. Do you know if there have been any in the area lately?" Maitland asked, glancing at his companions. "What? No one knows? Ah, well, I can always ask in town. Maybe someone has been carried off."

Only Tandry and Digby remained silent. While Tandry stared out the window as if he was contemplating some deep mystery, Digby held his head and groaned.

"Digby had another late night," Maitland said, following Annie's gaze. "He'd probably still be asleep if Snow White hadn't said that we needed to be here."

"Oh, good! Here's the food!" said Milo. "I'm so hungry I could eat a shark! I don't suppose you have any shark meat?" he asked the serving girl.

"Just kippers and whitefish, Your Highness," the girl replied. "I might be able to get you a good piece of eel tomorrow."

Nasheen was the first prince to leave the table. "I will go into town to find a way to be brave. Perhaps I will find a maiden in distress or hear of a monster terrorizing some local village. I am sure that I will come back victorious. Farewell, Your Majesty," he said, bowing to the king. "And Your Highness," he added, bowing to Snow White.

He had been gone only a few minutes when Liam joined them. "I've taken care of it," he whispered to Annie.

"Nasheen already left," Annie whispered back.

"Good," Liam told her. "There are guards waiting by the gate watching for the ones who leave early. They all volunteered, even Captain Sterling. They're tired of standing around watching for witches."

"Is everything all right?" asked Snow White.

Annie noticed that everyone was looking at them. She nodded and smiled. "Yes, of course. We were just talking about how much fun it will be to spend some time outside."

"That's what I was saying!" said Milo. "If you'll excuse me, I want to get started. I liked Maitland's idea. I'm going to look for a dragon!"

"Do you mind if I join you?" asked Andreas, following Milo to the door. "I've never hunted a dragon before."

Liam set some kippers and crusty bread on his plate as the other princes left the room. "That corridor is going to be crowded until they finish talking about what they're going to do. We might as well get something to eat while we wait for them to go. Here, these look good,"

165

he said as he passed a bowl of berries to Annie. "There's something I wanted to say," Liam told her. "Last night I thought about your contest for bravery. I don't know how well it's going to work. You can go about life and find yourself in a situation that requires bravery, but it would be much harder to go out looking for a situation that demands it—unless you actually find a dragon or manticore to fight, which isn't easy these days."

"I'm sure that's true, but Snow White didn't really have any choice. Her father has given her a short time to find a prince, certainly not enough time for a full-blown quest. And I'm sure that if the princes are intent on winning her hand, they'll figure something out."

Liam nodded. "Good enough."

"Are you really going to shoot at crows?" asked Annie as she helped herself to the berries.

"Later, when some of the princes get tired of stomping through the woods and come back to the castle," said Liam. "The number of crows seems to have doubled since yesterday. And you?"

"Horace and I are working on a project together. I'm hoping to finish it today."

"In that case, here's to a successful day!" Liam said, raising a tankard of cider.

৶

Annie was on her way to meet with Horace when she came across some of the ladies of the court she hadn't met before. There were only a few left on her list, so she was happy to have found them. Although she doubted that any of them was a witch in disguise, she pretended to bump into them just to make sure. The first two ladies were polite about it, but Annie knew they'd be whispering behind their hands as soon as they walked away. The third lady, who was by herself, was close to Annie's own age. When Annie bumped into her, the girl acted as if it was her own fault.

"I'm so sorry," the girl said, helping Annie to her feet. Annie's touch made the young lady's hair change from strawberry blond to flaming red, and freckles appeared on her cheeks and nose. If anything, Annie thought she was even prettier without the magic.

"It was my fault," said Annie. "I shouldn't have come around that corner so fast."

"Neither should I!" the girl said, laughing. "I have to say, it's so nice to have royalty visiting who behave like normal people. I probably shouldn't tell you this, but when Queen Marissa was here, we were all afraid of our shadows, the king was a ghost of himself, and no one ever laughed."

"That must have been awful!" said Annie. "I understand that a lot of people left then. If I might ask, why did you stay if it was so bad?"

The girl shrugged. "I didn't have anywhere else to go. My parents are dead, and the king is my godfather. Everyone is afraid that the queen is going to come back, but why would she with all these princes here ready to protect the castle?"

"Why indeed," said Annie. "I wonder . . . I have a project that I'm working on, and I could use your help. How would you like to play a role in a test for honesty?"

"You want to see how honest I am?"

"No, the test would be for Princess Snow White's suitors."

"What would I have to do?"

"It's very simple, really," said Annie. "You just have to drop a coin as you're walking away from a prince and see if he returns it to you. I'll have someone come watch so you'll know what the princes do with the coin if they don't give it back. When you're all finished, you tell me how everyone did."

"That sounds like fun!" the girl exclaimed. "I'd be happy to help. I'm Lady Cynara, by the way."

"And I'm Princess Annabelle."

"Everyone knows who you are!" said Cynara. "We know the names of all the princes, too. When would I start this test?"

"Whenever you want. I'll send someone around with the coins later today."

When Annie finally reached the office, Horace, Marta, and Tesia were already there, waiting for her. "I found a young lady who has agreed to help us with the honesty test," said Annie. "Lady Cynara is going to drop a coin and see if a prince returns it to her. I need some volunteers to watch from a hidden spot and see what the princes do."

"Spying on nobility! You'll have a lot of volunteers for that!" said Tesia.

After making plans for the honesty test, the two sisters left to bring more women to meet Annie. When every name was crossed off her list, she noticed that none of them had belonged to the girl who wore the furs.

"She works as a scullery maid," Marta told them, "so she should be in the kitchen, but no one has seen her today. No one seems to know her name, either. They just call her Hey You!"

"Please watch for her," said Annie. "We can't leave anyone out."

"Where to now, Your Highness?" asked Horace.

"I need to return to my chamber to get the coins for Lady Cynara. If you'll come with me, you can take them to her so she can start the honesty test."

"I wonder how those young princes are doing with their test for bravery," Horace said as they walked down the hall.

"I wonder if they've all left the castle yet. Some of them seemed to be having a difficult time making up their minds."

"Your Highness," a maid said, curtsying before Annie. "I have a message for you from a young man. He said to tell you that the person you're looking for is by the south tower right now, but might not be there long." Curtsying again, the girl scurried off.

"I guess I'm going to the south tower," said Annie. "Liam must have spotted the girl in the furs."

"Then it's good I'm still with you," Horace told her as he tried to keep up. "I don't want you meeting people alone, especially if she might be a fur-wearing, crow-loving witch!"

It took them longer than Annie would have liked to reach the south tower, which was at the far end of the castle, away from most of the day-to-day activity. Once they stepped outside, they didn't see anyone on their way there other than the guards on the tops of the walls, who seemed more interested in watching crows than people. The birds were perched on the tops of the towers, on the crenellations of the walls, and on the poles supporting the banners. A few crows circled the castle as if they were on patrol, watching everyone who came or went. Annie could feel their eyes on her as she crossed the open spaces. She was prepared to run if they came any closer, but none of them did.

The door to the tower was closed when they finally reached it, but it wasn't locked and they walked right in. "Is anyone here?" Annie called.

A shadow flitted across the far wall, but the person who cast it was out of sight. "I just want to talk to you!" cried Annie.

A door opened and closed somewhere ahead. Annie darted toward it.

"Wait!" Horace called, running after her.

Annie reached the door and stopped to peer inside. It was a long stairwell leading down, and the air wafting out of it smelled musty and damp. Torches lit the way, revealing moisture on the walls. Hearing the tap of feet on stone in front of her, Annie started down the stairs.

"I don't think this is a good idea," Horace called after Annie when he reached the top of the stairwell.

Annie wasn't so sure it was, either, but she was determined to talk to the elusive scullery maid. Only a few more steps and she'd be at the bottom of the stairs. She caught a glimpse of a dark-clad figure running ahead of her and through an open door.

"Hold up!" Horace shouted. "I'm coming!"

Annie ran across the short corridor and into a small, dark room. She stopped abruptly, looking for the person she'd been following. A moment later, Horace was there, huffing and puffing as he tried to catch his breath.

"Well, where is she?" he gasped, bent over with his hands resting on his knees.

"I don't know." Annie turned to look around the room. "Over there!" she cried as a heavy door, hidden in the gloom, ground shut. She darted toward it, but the floor was slippery, and the door closed before she could reach it. Hearing the grinding sound again, she turned in time to see the door through which they'd come close behind them as well.

"Well, isn't that just dandy," Horace said as they were plunged into darkness. "I hate to say it, Your Highness, but I think this was a trap."

"You think so?" Annie said, already mentally kicking herself. She started to walk toward the door and stubbed her toe on the uneven floor.

"Hold on a minute," said Horace. "I think I've got a flint here."

A gurgling sound started in one of the walls. Suddenly, water gushed from a series of holes and splashed onto the floor.

"It looks as if someone means to drown us!" said Horace. "I told you I didn't think coming down here was wise."

Annie shook her head even though he couldn't see her. "That isn't helping, Horace. Have you found that flint yet?"

"I know it's here somewhere. Ah, here it is! Now all we need is something to light."

"I don't think there are any torches on the walls," Annie said, straining to see in the absolute black of the room.

"I was thinking more of a stick or something."

"Would a handkerchief do?" she asked.

"It won't last long, but it's a start," said Horace.

Water was swirling around her ankles when Annie

waved the handkerchief toward where she'd last seen Horace.

"Say something so I know where you are," Horace told her.

"This water is cold," said Annie. "And it's awfully dark in here."

"I'm doing the best I can," said Horace.

"I'm talking so you can find me!"

"Oh, right. Do it again."

Instead, Annie began to sing, which wasn't easy because she was shivering so hard. The icy water was inching up to her knees, and she could hear Horace splashing as he stumbled around trying to find her. She flinched when he hit her arm.

"Here, I've got it," Horace said, his fumbling fingers taking the handkerchief from her hand.

She heard the sharp tap of the flint, but the spark was weak and went out right away. Suddenly, over the sound of the splashing water, there was a roar so loud and fierce that the entire room seemed to vibrate.

Annie's heart raced as she stared into the darkness, afraid of what she couldn't see. "What was that?" she asked.

"Sounded like a monster to me," said Horace.

Annie was incredulous. "You've got to be joking! First someone traps us in the dark and tries to drown us, then they send a monster after us? What's next, werewolves and dragons?"

"I don't think the monster is coming in here," said Horace. "Listen."

Staring into the dark was only making her imagine all sorts of dreadful things, so she closed her eyes and listened. There it was, a short, sharp sound like a dog barking. The monster roared again, and she could have sworn she heard people shouting.

"Is anyone out there?" Annie screamed, wading toward the sound. The water was up to her waist when she bumped into the door.

Horace stumbled against her, knocking her into the water. The old man grabbed the back of her gown and pulled her to her feet. "I thought maybe if we both yelled...," he said.

Annie was drenched from head to toe and shivering so hard that her teeth chattered, but she staggered toward the door and raised her voice to scream as loud as she could. "We're in here! Please help us!"

They were both pounding on the door and yelling when something banged against it on the other side. The barking was furious now, the roaring more frequent. Suddenly, the door slammed open and the water poured from the room, carrying Annie and Horace with it. They fell, swept headlong down the corridor, where they crashed into the first steps of the stairwell. For an instant, Horace was beside her, gasping like a beached fish, his eyes wide as the current dragged Annie away. When the monster roared again, the sound was almost deafening. Annie fought against the pull of the water, but before she could get her feet under her, something knocked her onto her back. A pair of enormous jaws closed around her middle even as she saw Liam lurch toward her, his sword raised high.

The crushing pressure on her back and stomach vanished. Something wiggled at her side. She looked down to find that a little lizard no longer than her hand had its tooth snagged on her sodden gown. The water was draining away when she sat up. Swiping her hair out of her eyes with one hand, she freed the lizard's tooth with the other and set the little creature on a stair. The last of the water trickled through cracks in the walls and floor as Annie got to her feet.

"Annie!" barked Dog, launching herself from the stairs.

She staggered under the dog's weight until she was able to brace her legs. "I'm happy to see you, too!" she said as Dog joyfully licked her face.

Horace groaned as he pulled himself onto a step. "Are you all right?" Annie asked him.

Dog left Annie to go nudge the old man.

"Fine as frog's hair," Horace gasped. He leaned against the wall, propping himself up with his arms. "I'm just not as young as I once was. This kind of thing takes a lot out of me."

"Annie," Liam said, and a moment later she was in his arms. After a quick hug, he held her at arm's length so he could look at her. "What about you? Did that monster hurt you?"

"That little lizard?" she asked, turning to watch it disappear into a crack in the wall.

"Actually, until it touched you, that little lizard was a three-headed monster as big as two warhorses," said Maitland, who was standing on a higher step. "The thing was covered in scales, had a thrashing tail longer than I am tall, and sharp teeth as big as my thumb."

Annie looked up. Captain Sterling was standing next to Maitland. Both men had torn clothes with blood on their arms and bodies, but neither one seemed to be badly injured. "Is that your blood or the monster's?" she asked.

The two men looked down at themselves and laughed. "The monster's," said the captain. "Prince Maitland cut off one of its heads to distract it while Prince Liam got past it and unbarred the door."

"Thank goodness you came when you did," Annie said, looking from one to the other but letting her eyes linger on Liam's face longer. "Horace and I would have drowned in there if not for you."

"Pardon me, Your Highness, but I would never have let that happen!" said Horace. "I was merely looking for the best way to free us from the witch's trap."

"And I'm sure you would have," said Liam, "if you hadn't drowned first!"

"How did you find us?" Annie asked him.

"Maitland and I were getting ready to shoot crows when we saw you two hurrying toward the south tower. I'd told you that I didn't want you going outside, so I knew it had to be something urgent to bring you here. Whatever it was, I didn't want you coming here without me, so Maitland and I followed you."

"Dog was with us and wanted to come, too. She was a big help tracking you once we were in the tower," said Maitland. "She led us to the stairs and warned us about the monster before we saw it. Liam and I were fighting the monster when Captain Sterling joined us, although I still don't know why he was there."

Annie glanced at the captain. He winked at her and said, "I just happened to be going this way." She smiled, remembering Liam telling her that the captain had volunteered to follow one of the princes. A draft made her shiver, and her teeth chattered loud enough for Liam to hear.

"You're freezing!" he exclaimed. "Let's get you out of here and somewhere warm and dry."

"What I'd really like is a hot bath!" said Annie.

"Haven't you had enough water?" Horace grumbled as Captain Sterling helped him to his feet. "I know I have."

The captain laughed and turned the old man toward the stairs. With Captain Sterling on one side and Maitland on the other, they helped Horace climb one step at a time. Dog ran ahead, running back to see them when they were too slow.

"Do you want me to carry you?" Liam asked Annie.

"I can manage," she said, smiling at him. They started up the stairs, which were wide enough that they could walk next to each other. "I have to tell you that I thought I was meeting you here. A maid brought a message telling me that the person I was looking for was in the tower, and that I should hurry because she wouldn't be here for long. She said that the person who sent the message was a man, so I thought it was you. Horace was already with me, so we came straight to the tower."

"A man, you say?" said Liam. "Then either he was working for the witch or we've been looking for the wrong person."

Maitland glanced at them over his shoulder. "I thought you were looking for Snow White's stepmother."

"We have been," Annie said. "But the crows are here, so I think Terobella might be as well. And that makes sense because when I met Queen Marissa, she had some magic, but she wasn't very powerful. Whoever turned that little lizard into a three-headed monster and those forest animals into wolves is a very powerful witch."

"I'm sure you're right," said Liam. "And I've been thinking about those crows. The last time we saw crows behaving oddly was when we were looking for the wicked fairy Voracia. She was talking to the roc skull about a horrible witch who had recently moved into her swamp. I think the witch's name might have been Terobella."

"Marissa and Terobella have to be working together," said Annie. "That room must be watertight without magic, because I touched those walls and they didn't start leaking. And if they were made to be water-tight, there has to be a nonmagical way to flood that room. Only someone like Marissa who knew the castle well would know about a room like that. The thing is, why would Terobella want to help anyone?"

"I don't think we'll know until we find them. But first things first," said Liam. "A hot bath should warm you up. Let me worry about finding the witches for now."

Liam left Annie at her door and went off to tell some-one to bring her enough hot water to fill a tub. While she was waiting for the water, she took off her still-dripping clothes and wrapped herself in one of Snow White's soft robes. When she finally heard a knock on the door, she opened it to find a slew of maids carrying buckets brimming with steaming water. Another round of maids came, and the tub was full. Alone at last, she lowered herself into the tub and leaned back, relaxing as the water warmed her.

Annie was more than half asleep by the time the water had cooled enough to wake her. She was still cold and tired, so she pulled on a warm nightgown and crawled under the bedcovers. Normally she felt guilty for taking a nap in the middle of the day when she knew she had lots to do, but this had been no ordinary day.

CHAPTER 14

AN INSISTENT BANGING on her chamber door finally woke Annie.

"I thought you might take a nap," Liam said when she answered the door, clutching the robe around her. "I would have let you sleep until tomorrow, but I thought you'd want to hear the princes tell how brave they were today."

"Oh, that's right! I almost forgot. I'll be ready in a few minutes!" she said, closing the door.

Annie had gotten used to dressing herself without a maid's help long ago and could do it quickly now. Rummaging through the clothes in a wardrobe, she found a simple gown elegant enough to wear to supper with the king. She didn't want to take the time to put her hair up, so she tried braiding it on one side of her head to cover the hair that had been burned. Satisfied with her reflection in the mirror, she finished braiding her hair as she left the room and joined Liam in the corridor.

Although there were still a few people hurrying toward the great hall, nearly everyone was already there. King Archibald was coming down the corridor when Annie and Liam entered the hall. As soon as the king took his seat, servers started bringing in the food. Unlike the night before, the princes looked pleased with themselves, and none of them showed signs of being nervous. They hurried through the roasted boar, the eel stew, and the trout wrapped in bacon, wolfing down great quantities as if they hadn't eaten in days.

The king watched his daughter's suitors in amusement, asking if anyone was still hungry when they slowed. After they'd assured him that they couldn't eat another bite, he turned to Snow White and said, "Then it's time for you to hear what they have to say."

"My cousin Emilio and I would like to go first, if we may," said Cozwald. "You all know what we did today," he said, glancing at the other contestants. "We asked each of you to join us, but no one did, so we held our own jousting tournament. We fought quite bravely, unseating each other and each winning our own fair share of rounds."

"That we did," said Emilio. "I don't see how anyone could have been braver."

Snow White nodded. "Very good," she said. "I wish I could have seen it."

"Milo and I also worked together today," said Andreas.

"We went dragon hunting!" exclaimed Milo. "We found trees that a dragon had scorched with its flames and followed them to the dragon's lair!"

"We went inside, armed with swords and spears," said Andreas, "but the dragon hid in the depths of its cave, so frightened at our brave appearance that it refused to come out."

Milo nodded. "We would have stayed to taunt it into fighting, but we knew that we had to get back here in time for supper to tell you of our deeds."

"Bravely done!" said Snow White. "I've never had anyone fight dragons in my name before."

"And she still hasn't," Liam muttered to Annie.

"You tasted the fruits of my labors today," announced Tandry. "I went hunting for wild boar and killed the ferocious beast that attacked me. I brought back its carcass and gave it to your cooks. We ate it roasted for supper tonight."

"That was the boar you killed?" said Snow White. "That's wonderful! You must have been very brave!"

"I can't wait to hear what really happened," Liam whispered to Annie. "I've never heard of a mystic who liked to hunt."

"He never said he was a mystic," Annie whispered to him.

"Maybe not," said Liam. "But I think he wants to

look like one. Have you noticed how often he pretends to meditate?"

"Maybe he really is," said Annie, glancing at Tandry again.

"Then he needs to make up his mind. He sounded awfully bloodthirsty for a mystic!"

"I fought a man twice my size today," said Nasheen. "He was a bully, terrorizing the people of your little town. After I thrashed him soundly, he fled and will not be back soon, I think."

"Do you know the man's name?" Liam asked.

"I believe I heard someone call him Fitchfield," said Nasheen.

King Archibald's eyebrows shot up.

"Do you know this man, Your Majesty?" asked Maitland.

"I have heard of him," said the king.

"Then you know what a service I have done for your kingdom!" Nasheen said, sounding exultant.

King Archibald turned a very odd look on Nasheen. He opened his mouth as if he had something to say, then stopped and shook his head.

"And what about you, Digby?" asked Annie. "What did you do today?"

"I rescued a damsel in distress," said Digby. "At great personal risk, I might add. I carried her from a burning building to safety."

"Really! Then it was very fortunate for this girl that you were there!" Snow White told him.

"And you, Maitland," said Nasheen. "What was your brave act?"

Maitland turned to Snow White. "I helped Liam rescue Annie from drowning."

"What?" she exclaimed. "Annie, what is he talking about?"

"It's true," Annie said. "Horace and I were led to a room in the south tower and locked inside. Whoever led us there flooded the room. It was Liam who unbarred the door, but it was Maitland who—"

"Liam is the real hero of this story, Annie," said Maitland.

"But you were there, and you—"

"Don't deserve the credit," Maitland said, asking her to stop with a pleading look.

Annie sat back in her seat and pursed her lips. Being humble was one thing, but now was not the time!

Snow White gave them each a puzzled look, but it was her father who said, "That will be enough for tonight! We have heard some excellent stories of bravery, and tomorrow night we shall hear stories of a different sort. I'm sure you are all tired and could use a good night's rest before your next trial. We will meet at eight o'clock tomorrow morning, when my daughter will announce the last of the tests. Good night, gentlemen."

The king stood and left the room, taking Snow White with him and leaving the princes to talk among themselves.

"That has to be the most trumped-up story I've ever heard," said Nasheen. "A room filling with water! And Maitland just happened to be there! Tell us what really happened, Maitland. Or were your friends making up a story for you because you did nothing at all today? Is that why you didn't want to talk about it?"

"I believe I am tired and will follow King Archibald's suggestion," Maitland said as he pushed his chair back. "Good night, everyone. I'll see you in the morning."

"Coward!" Nasheen spat as Maitland walked away.

Maitland's back stiffened, but he paused for only a moment before leaving the hall.

"A wise man does not make unfounded judgments," Liam said, glaring at Nasheen. "Princess Annabelle does not lie, nor does she make up stories to boost anyone's ego. You insulted her when you questioned him, and I do not take it kindly. You owe the princess an apology!"

"I did not mean to impugn the princess's character," said Nasheen, "but that story—"

"Was only part of the real story, which is even harder to believe," said Annie.

"Then I apologize for my remarks!" Nasheen said through stiff lips.

"The one you really need to apologize to is Prince

Maitland!" said Annie. "If not for him, I might not be here this evening! Whatever the reason for his humility, it is not for you or any of us to judge him."

"My lady," Liam said, getting to his feet and setting his hand on the back of her chair.

Annie stood, and together they walked from the hall while the princes watched them in silence.

"We're supposed to meet Snow White and her father in the small dining hall to hear the guards' reports," Liam told Annie, hurrying her down the corridor.

Annie smiled up at Liam and squeezed his hand. "You really told Nasheen!"

"I try to be impartial when I meet people, but I don't like that man," said Liam. "He thinks too highly of himself and not enough of the people he should respect."

"Maybe he's a good person when he's not competing for a princess's hand," Annie told him.

"Maybe he is," said Liam. "But I doubt it!"

They entered the small dining hall to find it nearly full. The king and Snow White were there, as were the eight guards who had followed the princes throughout the day.

"I must say, the princes' stories were very interesting," declared King Archibald as he turned to Liam.

"If Your Majesty wouldn't mind, could you tell us about the man Nasheen encountered?" asked Liam.

"I met Fitchfield once, but I've heard much about him. He's a good, honest man, which is why I employ him as a tax collector. Fitchfield is not a bully. I know because I keep an eye out for that kind of thing. He is a large man, so Prince Nasheen was correct when he said that the man is twice his size. Unfortunately, that was the only true thing he said. I'll have to send one of my men out to make sure Fitchfield is all right."

"He is, Your Majesty," said one of the guards. "I was the one who followed Prince Nasheen today, and I can tell you exactly what happened. Nasheen went into the city looking for a fight. He entered a tavern called the Rusty Sword and insulted two men, who left rather than fight him. The way he was dressed, it was obvious he was nobility, and nobody wants to brawl with them, pardon me for saying. Then he went down the street and found Master Fitchfield eating his midday meal at the tavern called the Golden Swan. He was talking to a merchant who had stopped by for a friendly chat. The two men obviously knew each other and were engaged in the kind of ribbing my mates and me give each other all the time. Nasheen purposely misunderstood and hauled Fitchfield out of his chair, drubbed him soundly, and threw him into the street. When the prince started bragging about what he had done, nobody would listen to him, seeing that they all like Fitchfield. The tavern keeper took Fitchfield into a back room to clean him up, but the prince was too busy talking about himself to notice. I checked on your tax collector before I left. The man is going to be fine."

"Thank you for that," said the king. "I'll have the court physician look at him anyway. Now, what about Prince Digby? I haven't heard of a fire in the city."

"It wasn't much of a fire," said another guard. "Digby went into the Slippery Eel and knocked over a candle. The greasy tabletop caught on fire. When the barmaid started screaming, Digby threw her over his shoulder and ran out of the tavern. The owner of the Slippery Eel slapped the table with his apron until he put out the fire, but by then Digby was gone and didn't pay his bill."

"My, how a story can change," said Snow White.

Captain Sterling nodded to the guard next to him, who cleared his throat and said, "I followed Prince Andreas, and Pelty there followed Prince Milo. They went for a ride in the woods and were taking potshots at squirrels when they came across a lightning-struck tree. They both started talking about dragons then. After that, they rode around some more until they found a small cave."

"They went inside and were out of sight for about a minute, then they came back out talking about how the dragon must be hiding," said the guard named Pelty. "After they rode off, I went in the cave. It was about ten feet deep without any openings in the back. There was no way a dragon would have used that cave."

"Milo and Andreas must have good imaginations," said Snow White. "What about Tandry?"

"Prince Tandry went hiking in the woods by himself and eventually did find a wild boar," said the guard who had followed him. "However, he was not well prepared. When he actually stumbled on the boar, he ran at it with a spear. The boar turned on him, and Tandry dropped the spear so he could climb the nearest tree. He stayed in the tree until the boar wandered off, whereupon the prince returned to the city. On the way back, he stopped at a farm and bought a freshly slaughtered pig, which he brought to the castle."

"So the pork we ate at supper tonight wasn't wild at all," said Liam.

"And Tandry lied," Snow White said, scowling. "That wasn't just an overactive imagination, like it was with Milo and Andreas."

"At least we know that Cozwald and Emilio really did have a tournament," said Annie.

"That's true," said Liam. "I caught a glimpse of them jousting in the fields outside the south wall. What can you tell us about that?" he asked the two guards who hadn't spoken yet.

One of the men tried not to smile when he said, "Just that they competed all afternoon, and neither one is very good."

"If they were that bad, I think they were brave for trying," said Snow White.

"And now for Maitland," said Annie. "I don't know

why he didn't want to tell what really happened, because he was extraordinarily brave."

"I couldn't have opened the door to let Annie and the water out if Maitland hadn't cut off one of the monster's heads," said Liam.

"A monster in my castle!" exclaimed the king.

"What monster?" said Snow White.

"How many heads did it have?" asked one of the guards.

"It was a three-headed monster, Your Majesty," said Captain Sterling. "It had been put there to guard the door to a room in the lower level of the south tower. We could hear water running behind the door. When we realized that Princess Annabelle and Horace were locked in the room, Maitland and I distracted the monster so that Prince Liam could get past. We both fought the monster, but Maitland was able to get close enough to cut off one of its heads. He is very good with a sword and a fearless fighter. If it's a brave man you are looking for, Your Highness, he would be an excellent choice. He's the kind of man I wouldn't mind having by my side in any battle."

"Oh my!" said Snow White. "I wish he had told me."

"Perhaps he's also a modest man?" Annie suggested.

"Thank you, Captain Sterling," said King Archibald. "You have been of great service."

"You're most welcome, Your Majesty. We were honored to be of assistance," replied the captain.

"We're going to need you to follow the princes again tomorrow," Annie told him.

The guards' eyes lit up, and they looked at one another and smiled. As Captain Sterling and his men left the room, Liam leaned toward Annie and said, "Apparently they like spying on the princes better than standing around doing nothing."

The king had already stood, and Liam got up to talk to him.

"Can you blame them when most of the princes are making fools of themselves?" Snow White said to Annie. "I'm glad you thought to send the guards to watch them, Annie, or I might never have learned the truth."

"And Maitland . . . ," said Annie.

"I think I know why he didn't want to talk about what he did," said Snow White. "He told me that he thinks this is all a game and that I deserve better than this. He says that these princes can't possibly know me well enough to love me the way he does. He doesn't like competing with them, but he will because I said he must. He said that he would do his best, but that he wouldn't want to sing his own praises, because it would make him feel like he was giving the game more value than it warrants."

"I didn't know he was so romantic," said Annie.

"I didn't, either," said Snow White. "I think I misjudged him. When he was here before, he seemed so arrogant, and I was furious when I heard what he'd said to his friends."

"What did he say?" said Annie. "You never did tell me."

Snow White pursed her lips, and her eyes flicked away, then back to Annie. Her voice was rough when she said, "He told them that marrying me was the solution to his problems. He said that he'd asked around, and not only was I the king's only child, I was his only living relative. If Maitland married me, he'd get a beautiful wife and his own kingdom to rule. Beldegard could keep Montrose. Helmswood was just as good, and the king was so old and frail that he probably wouldn't last long. I was furious when I heard him, and it's taken me a long time to see that it wasn't the real Maitland talking; it was a young man trying to impress his friends. Now I think the real Maitland is a very different person. I only wish I could look at him without remembering what he said."

"Are you ready, ladies?" Liam asked from the doorway.

Annie looked up. The king had already gone, and Liam was obviously waiting for them. "Do you think you'll make up your mind about Maitland soon?" she asked Snow White.

"I hope so," said Snow White as she started toward the door.

After saying good night to Snow White, Liam escorted Annie to her chamber. "I have a question for you," she said when they were alone in the corridor. "Why was Maitland with you when you saw Horace and me? Why wasn't he out looking for some way to show his bravery?"

"Maitland told me that he had tried to think of the thing he feared the most so he could go face it in Snow White's name. He said that the only thing he could come up with was that Snow White would turn him down after he told her how much he loved her. He'd already decided to go see her and propose again when we saw you and Horace."

"I'm sorry he missed his chance to propose," said Annie.

Liam smiled. "Oh, I don't doubt that he'll try again."

CHAPTER 15

ANNIE WOKE the next morning to the sound of flapping wings. She sat up, startled, and looked toward the window. A crow had landed on the ledge and was peering into the room with its little button eyes, tilting its head from one side to the other. When she moved again, it saw her, squawked, and flew away.

It was only a little earlier than Annie normally got up, so she threw back the covers and crawled to the edge of the bed. She shivered when her feet touched the cold floor. Wrapping the robe around herself, she padded to the window and looked out. There were more crows today than there had been the day before. As Annie watched, a group rose from the top of one building and flew to another. She shivered again, but this time it wasn't from the cold.

☙

Annie wasn't the only one who was early for breakfast that morning. Snow White and Maitland were standing by the table, talking, but when Annie entered the room, they stepped apart and took their regular seats. Liam and the other princes soon drifted in, and they all seemed to be in good spirits. Even Tandry, who normally seemed distracted, smiled when he saw Snow White.

As soon as the king took his seat, Snow White stood and announced, "We're going to eat first today. I don't want any of you running off before you've had a good, hearty breakfast."

Servers began bringing in large bowls of blueberries and cut-up melon, oatcakes and honey, eggs fried in butter, and slices of spiced ham. The princes took great, heaping platefuls and ate without talking, draining their mugs of cider over and over again. When everyone had finished, Snow White stood.

"Today's test is not a difficult one," she told them. "All you have to do is show me that you are capable of compassion. I will hear your stories after supper this evening. I hope you all have a good day and find this test easy."

"Compassion?" said Milo once Snow White and the king had left the room. "I don't understand. What does she want us to do?"

"I believe the princess wants us to help someone in some way," said Maitland.

Emilio nodded. "I think she means that we should do good deeds."

"That's easy enough," said Cozwald. "I do those all the time."

"Then I'll meet you back here this afternoon, cousin," said Emilio, "after we've done our good deeds for the day."

"What do *you* plan to do today?" Annie asked Liam as the others left the room.

"I'm going to spend the day searching for the witches." He slipped the last oatcake in his pocket, saying, "Dog would like this."

"There's something I should have told you before this, but I thought you would tell me not to do it," said Annie. "It's just that I was sure it was such a good idea and was bound to work. It didn't, though, and, well, I think I should tell you about it anyway.... Remember how I went up to all the young women at the ball when I was looking for the girl that the fairy Moonbeam was helping? I've tried to do the same thing here to find the witches. I've gone up to all the noblewomen as well as the women who work here. Not one of them is a witch."

"I know," said Liam. "Horace told me all about it."

"He did!" Annie exclaimed. "When did he do that?"

"The first day. He had volunteered to follow you to make sure you were safe, so when you and Snow White started approaching the ladies of the court, he told me what you were doing."

"He's very good at staying out of sight," said Annie. "I had no idea he was there. How is he doing now? He didn't look at all well after we got out of that horrible room with all the water."

"He'll be fine. Sterling is making him rest." Liam grinned at Annie. "You know, you made it much easier on the old fellow when you asked for his help. When you met with the women in that office, I had two men stationed outside the door in case you actually found Queen Marissa. I thought it was more likely that the witches were posing as serving girls, or maids, or even cooks in the kitchen, than women of nobility, and I didn't want you at the witch's mercy if you did find one."

"I never knew," said Annie, feeling a little foolish. For someone who was trying to find someone who didn't want to be found, she hadn't been very observant. "Why are you looking for the witches yourself today? If I couldn't find them, what makes you think that you can?"

"Because I'm not going to look for women who are living openly in the castle," Liam said. "I'm going to look for witches hiding in dark corners somewhere out of the way, just as we hunted for the evil fairy before your sister's sixteenth birthday."

"Ah!" said Annie. "Do you need my help?"

"Probably, but I have a few things to do first. I'm taking Dog and some guards. We'll come get you when we're ready."

Annie watched as Liam headed for the great hall. His answer had surprised her; she hadn't expected him to say that she could join him. It had taken a while, but she'd finally realized that he became angry with her because he feared for her safety. Apparently, he was less afraid of facing a horrible monster than he was of seeing something bad happen to her. If he was going to let her join him in his search for the witch, he must have something in mind that he hadn't told her about.

Annie turned toward the kitchen. She was still determined to talk to the fur-wearing scullery maid, and the kitchen was the only place where she thought she might find her.

The kitchen was a large room with fireplaces and a huge wood-burning oven set into the wall at one end. Located partway below ground level, it was a nest of activity with all the cooks and their helpers scurrying around. While some cleaned up from breakfast, others were already preparing the next meal, washing vegetables, cutting up haunches of meat, and taking round loaves of bread out of the oven.

Annie stood for a moment, looking for the fur-wearing girl. When a cook noticed Annie, she stopped giving orders to her helpers and curtsied. In an instant, everyone else was curtsying as well.

"Your Highness," said the cook. "How may we help you?"

"I'm looking for one of your scullery maids. The one who wears furs," said Annie.

The cook looked around until someone piped up, "She left just a minute ago to fetch more eggs for the cake."

"She's gone outside," said the cook.

"Thank you," Annie replied, and started toward the door.

Everyone watched in silence as Annie walked the length of the kitchen. She was closing the door behind her when she heard someone say, "Now, what do you suppose a princess wants with the likes of Hey You?"

Annie stood just inside the door, not sure if she really wanted to step outside. Liam had been adamant that she stay indoors, and she did think that the crows were waiting for their chance to come after her. She was holding the door open a crack when she saw a figure moving between the outbuildings. Certain that she might not have another opportunity to talk to the girl, she pushed the door back and hurried across the open space. When she saw the girl enter a long, low building filled with clucking, rustling chickens, Annie followed her inside. She was about to call out when a rooster burst from a group of hens and rushed toward her.

"Grab the broom!" shouted the scullery maid. "Whack him with it if he gets close!"

Annie looked around. Spotting an old broom leaning against the wall, she grabbed it and held it with both hands. When the rooster launched himself from the dirt floor with his spurred legs aimed at her, she swatted the broom at him, knocking him to the side.

"Good one!" shouted the scullery maid as the rooster landed on the ground with a squawk. "I couldn't have done better myself! Hold on to that for now. He may come back."

Annie and the bird watched each other warily as he righted himself. Chickens pecked and scratched at the ground, crowding around her feet.

"Did you come here for a reason or just to see the birds?" asked the scullery maid.

"I came to see you, actually," said Annie.

Now it was the girl's turn to look wary. She held her basket in front of herself in a protective gesture and said, "Why? What do you want?"

Annie sighed. She was tired of wondering if every woman she met might be a witch. And she was tired of worrying that she might actually find the witch who wanted to kill her and not have any defense against whatever she tried to do. It occurred to her that she'd been foolish to follow anyone to an isolated coop, but after meeting the girl, she really didn't think she was a witch. She doubted very much that the witch would actually do any real labor, or dress in such obviously uncomfortable clothes.

"I just want to touch your hand, and then I'll leave you alone," said Annie.

"Why? What will that do? I know people have been going to see you, but nobody says why, at least not when I've been around."

"I'm just trying to make sure that everyone is who they say they are."

"And what if I don't want you to touch me?" asked the girl.

Annie blinked. No one had refused her touch before, and she certainly didn't want to force the girl. "I just want to touch your hand," said Annie. "I'm not going to hurt you!"

"What exactly are you looking for?"

"Oh, for goodness' sake!" Annie said. "I want to make sure you aren't a witch pretending to be someone who is supposed to live here."

"Is that all! Well, in that case, here," the girl said, thrusting her hand toward Annie.

The moment the girl was close enough for Annie to get a good look at her, it became obvious that she was no ordinary scullery maid. Although her furs were filthy and smelled horrible, her face and hands were smeared with dried dirt, and her hair was an uncombed, unwashed rat's nest, Annie could tell that under it all she was undeniably beautiful. Touching her hand diminished her beauty, but not by much. "You're a princess, aren't you!" exclaimed Annie. "What on earth are you doing here?"

Snatching her hand back, the girl tucked it behind

her. "Why would you say such a ridiculous thing? Look at me! How could I possibly be a princess?"

"You're dressed like that because you don't want people to know who you are!" Annie exclaimed. "That's some disguise, although I can't imagine why anyone would go to such lengths. Don't worry," she said, seeing how fearful the girl had become. "Your secret is safe with me!"

"How can you tell?" asked the girl. "No one else has ever looked past the dirt or the furs."

"I suppose it's because I'm used to looking for the real person behind the magic, or mud, for that matter," said Annie. "Why are you here, dressed like this?"

"I'm hiding from my father," the girl replied. "He's a king across the sea, but even here he has friends who would be happy to return me to him. I left the kingdom a few months ago when I turned sixteen, the day after he announced that he was going to make me marry his best friend, a cruel, old man with a shriveled heart and no hair except for the tufts in his ears. I left as soon as I knew and hid in a ship that brought me to Gulleer. I made this disguise and came here by foot after I saw one of my father's friends near the docks. Did you mean it when you said that you wouldn't tell?"

"I promise!" said Annie. "But Snow White and her father would help you if they only knew."

"Then others would find out, word would spread, and my father would come after me!" the girl cried.

"No one needs to know who you really are, but you should at least come up with a name that people can call you. I was told that everyone here refers to you as Hey You! Can't you think of another name?"

"I've always liked the name Lilah," she said.

"I like that!" said Annie. "I'm Annie, by the way."

"Princess Annabelle, you mean," said Lilah. "Everyone in the castle knows who you are. You're engaged to that handsome Prince Liam."

"I am," Annie said with a smile. "Speaking of Liam, I'd better get back. He'll be looking for me soon. I'm glad I got to meet you, Lilah. If I can help you in any way, let me know."

"I will," Lilah said. "And thank you!"

As Annie left the chicken coop, she was thinking about what she could do to help the unfortunate princess and didn't notice the crows until the sky overhead blackened and the first of the birds descended on her. When one flew at her head, she threw up her arm, forgetting that she was still holding the broom. The crow veered away, but others came at her to beat their wings in her face, reaching with their gripping, tearing claws and snapping beaks.

Annie screamed and flailed at the crows with the broom, ducking her head when they got too close. She was fighting them off when Lilah appeared, tossing her stinky, dirt-encrusted cape over Annie's head.

"Run!" Lilah shouted. "There's a door over here!"

With Lilah guiding her, Annie ran to the closest door. Lilah flung it open, and they both dashed inside, slamming the door in the faces of more than a dozen crows. As the crows screeched their displeasure, Annie turned to Lilah. "Thank you so much for helping me! I'd still be out there trying to get away if you hadn't come to my rescue."

"I'm glad I could help!" said Lilah. "That could have been really nasty."

After handing the broom to Lilah, Annie pulled off the cape and handed her that as well. "Ouch!" Annie said when the cape touched one of the scrapes on her wrists. "I don't understand. The crows didn't bother me at all yesterday, but today they're awful. I wonder why?"

"I've never seen birds act like that," said Lilah. "Did you do something to make them angry?"

"No, although it seems that the witch who controls them doesn't like me one bit. I need to go now. Thanks again for helping me."

"That's quite all right," said Lilah.

❧

Annie examined the cuts and scrapes on her hands and wrists on the way back to her chamber. Her hair was a tangled mess when she brushed it back from her face, and she knew she smelled, both from wearing the cape and from contact with the crows. When she saw a footman on her way down the corridor, she sent for bathwater, and asked him to hurry.

Opening the door to her chamber, Annie paused for a moment at the threshold. Something was wrong, but she wasn't sure what it might be. The room was on the west side of the castle and wouldn't benefit from direct sunlight until later in the day. There was light from the windows, of course, but the room was still gloomy with deep shadows in the corners and above the bed's high canopy. There was a musky smell, though, one that hadn't been there before, as if some great mangy beast had taken up residence under her bed.

"What is that?" Annie murmured as she stepped into the room and closed the door behind her. She was still trying to place the smell when something moved on top of the canopy. Annie glanced up and was startled to find crows perched there, watching her. A tiny skittering sound drew her gaze to the wardrobe placed against the back wall. Two crows were perched there as well. When she heard a sound behind her, she spun on her heel and found a row of crows atop the doorframe only a few feet away.

The room was silent until a crow near one of the windows cried, "Caw!"

Suddenly, the air outside her windows filled with crows. They poured through the openings like a flood of black water. Annie stood, frozen for a heartbeat, then flung herself at the door, wrenching it open even as the crows that had been perched on the doorframe flew at her. One beat its wings in her face, but like the crow at the tower where they'd left Granny Bentbone, the moment it touched her, the witch's control over it vanished, leaving the bird confused. Annie screamed, as much in surprise as in fear, and the crow flew out the window. There were others to take its place, however, and a whole stream of crows followed her into the corridor.

Annie slammed the door, but crows were already there, tearing at her arms with their beaks and claws as she tried to protect her face and eyes. Each time a crow touched her, it left the fray, flapping aimlessly around the corridor as if it wasn't sure why it was there. Finally there was only one crow left. Ignoring the searing pain as it ripped at her arms with its claws, Annie grabbed it by a wing and whirled, smashing the bird against the wall. The black form slid to the floor, limp, while the other crows flew down the corridor to the nearest window. The birds inside her room hurled themselves against the stout wooden door with enough force to shake it.

Within moments the corridor was filled with running guards and people from the rooms near hers, summoned by her screams. Maitland, whose room was only a few doors away, tore past them all. "Annie! What happened? Your arms..."

"I'll be all right," Annie said, although she was

shaking and suddenly felt cold and clammy. Blood dripped down her arm when she pointed at her door. "My room is filled with crows. That one attacked me." When she pointed at the crow on the floor, the people standing near it stepped back.

"Let me see that," Maitland said, taking a clean handkerchief from his pocket and wrapping it around Annie's wrist where the bleeding was the worst. "You!" he barked at one of the guards. "Take Princess Annabelle to Princess Snow White's chamber, and then fetch the royal physician. You and you, come with me," he said, pointing at other guards. "And you, lend me your sword."

The first guard was already helping Annie down the corridor when Maitland and the two men ran into Annie's chamber. They fought the crows back as they entered the room, then the door shut, muffling the sounds.

When Snow White opened her door, the overpowering scent of flowers wafted into the corridor. The princess looked surprised to see Annie with a guard, but the moment she saw her friend's wounds she pulled her into the room and sent the guard after the physician. Annie swallowed hard. The chamber was filled with bouquets of wildflowers as well as flowers from the castle's own garden. Her stomach was queasy, and the smell was only making it worse.

"Here, sit down," said Snow White. "You look as if you're going to fall over."

She was heading toward the window seat when Annie shook her head and said, "Not there. Not by the window. I don't want the crows to see me!"

"All right," Snow White said, taking her to the chair by the table instead. "Can I get you something to drink?"

Annie shook her head. "I couldn't. My stomach is upset."

Snow White frowned, concern written on her face. She touched Annie's cheek and her frown deepened. "Maybe you should lie down."

"I couldn't," said Annie. "I'll bleed all over your lovely covers."

"Don't you worry about that!" Snow White exclaimed. "Friends are more important than covers. I lived with seven dwarves long enough to know a bit about medicine. Working in a mine is a dangerous business, and one or another of them was always getting hurt. I could treat this myself if I was at the cottage with my herbs handy, but we'll have to wait until the physician comes now. I've never met him, but any healer worth his salt will have what I need. Lie down on the bed while I get some clean cloths. We can do that much for the bleeding at least. This should work," she said, taking a fine soft shift from a trunk and ripping it into pieces. Annie cried out in protest when she saw what her friend had done.

Snow White brought a bowl of clean water and one of the strips of cloth to Annie's side and began to clean her wounds. When Annie drew back, Snow White began to talk in a cheerful voice as if to distract her. "Did I tell you what my suitors have been up to? They've all been bringing me flowers. Digby brings me bouquets that look just like the ones the head gardener normally sends to my room every morning. Nasheen drops off one perfect blossom from the castle garden, while Emilio collects flowers from the swamp just past the village. Milo makes wreaths for my hair. He ties the stems together with the most intricate knots. They're really quite lovely."

"Ouch!" cried Annie as Snow White cleaned one of the deeper wounds. "Go on!" she said through gritted teeth. "What else have they done?"

Snow White continued to talk as she fetched the other scraps of fabric. "Let's see…Nasheen took me riding this morning. He gave me a few pointers, then rode off at a gallop. I couldn't keep up, and when he disappeared and didn't come back, I waited for a while. I finally returned to the castle without him. The mare he gave me is very nice, although I don't think much of Nasheen as a riding instructor."

Annie laughed, but it turned into a groan when Snow White began to wrap a bandage around her wrist.

"Tandry brought me a sack with a dead rabbit in it," Snow White hurried to say when Annie grimaced at the pain. "He said he would get me one every day if I liked. I thanked him and asked him to take the rest to the kitchen."

"Tandry doesn't seem to know much about choosing gifts for a lady," said Annie.

"Ah, but then there's Andreas. He tried to serenade me last night, but he picked the wrong window and sang to an elderly noblewoman instead. She told me this morning that she thinks she's in love."

Annie was laughing again when there was a knock on the door, and Snow White called out, "What is it?"

"Flowers for you, Your Highness," said the voice. "They're from Prince Tandry this time."

"Give them to someone else!" called Snow White. "I have too many in here as it is. And let it be known that I don't want to be disturbed for the rest of the day." Snow White glanced at Annie's face. Pressing her palm to Annie's forehead, she clucked her tongue and said, "You're too pale, and your skin is cool and damp. Lie still while I raise your feet." She shoved a pillow under Annie's legs.

"I don't want—" Annie began.

"And this blanket should keep you warm."

"But I—" Annie protested.

The door slammed open and suddenly Liam was there. "I heard you were hurt, Annie. What happened?"

Annie sat up suddenly, which made her head spin. "I'm all right. Just a few cuts—"

"If only I had some yarrow!" said Snow White. "Where is that physician?"

Liam sat down beside Annie. "He's coming. I saw him in the corridor just now."

"I should always keep my herbs at hand. Perhaps I'll start an herb garden here," Snow White said to herself.

"Where's my patient?" the physician demanded as he bustled into the room. He was an older man with a round belly and a round face, and he exuded confidence as he stopped in front of Annie. A young man scurried in behind him, carrying a large leather bag. "Now, what have we here?" the physician said.

"Do you have yarrow with you?" Snow White asked him.

"I'm not an herbalist, Your Highness. I practice only the most modern medicine. Unwrap those bandages, young man, and let me take a look. My, those are deep. Well, these bandages will do. We'll just wrap them up again, and ... Boy, where are my leeches?" he said, turning to his helper.

"Why do you need leeches?" asked Liam. "She's already bleeding!"

"Remove the bad humors, young man," said the physician. "Always a good idea!"

Snow White stepped between Annie and the royal physician. "You are not using leeches on her! You're finished here. Out! Out right now! Guard, make sure this man leaves," she told the guard who had brought the physician. "Annie, I'm going to go look for yarrow, and I'll…wait a moment! I might already have some!" she said when her eyes landed on a bouquet of wildflowers.

The physician stared at Snow White openmouthed as she hurried across the room. "Well, I never!" he said, shoving the jar of leeches back in his leather sack. "King Archibald will hear about this!"

"And from more than one person," said Liam, taking Annie's hand in his. "Don't worry, that man isn't coming anywhere near you."

Only moments after the physician stormed out, Snow White stood up from where she was bent over the bouquet, waving some white blossoms in the air. "This should do the trick," she said. Taking a clean goblet from the table, she tore up some of the yarrow leaves and mashed them into a paste. After removing the bandages, she spread the paste on the still-bleeding wounds. Within minutes, the bleeding stopped.

"Leeches!" she muttered under her breath. "I'm going to plant a *big* herb garden."

"Thank you, Snow White." said Annie. "It already hurts less."

Liam leaned down to kiss Annie's forehead. "Good! I was going to ask if you wanted to come with me now, but I think you should stay here and rest."

"Oh no!" Annie said. "You can't look for the witch by yourself. What if she tries to use magic on you?"

"We'll just have to be faster than she is," Liam replied.

"I don't like this one bit! If you go without me and you meet the witch, she'll have gotten exactly what she wanted! I won't be there to protect you, and she could turn you into a snail or something. Snow White, you have to help me convince him!"

"Annie is right," said Snow White. "I'm sure the witch would love to get rid of you. If you aren't around, Annie will be vulnerable to whatever the witch has planned. It's still early. Can't you wait until Annie has rested for a bit? I can give her some tincture of valerian to help her take a nap. I might have a bloom or two, and if I don't, I'm sure I can find some growing near the castle."

Liam reached down to brush a loose tendril from Annie's cheek. "I'll wait, but if you aren't up to it later, I'll have to go without you."

"I'll be ready," said Annie. "You'll see."

CHAPTER 16

"WE FOUND YOU a new room," Liam told Annie as she tidied her hair. She felt much better after her nap and was glad Snow White had persuaded Liam to wait.

"Was my old room in such terrible shape?" she asked.

"Yes, it was. Plus Maitland and I didn't want you where the crows could find you again. Your new room is smaller, and we've covered the window with a tapestry so the crows can't look in and see you."

"If I'm in the only room with the window covered, won't the witches suspect something?"

"We thought of that," Liam said with a grin. "So we had a lot of windows covered. We're ready to go now. Are you?"

"Who's 'we'?" asked Annie.

"Quite a group, actually. Captain Sterling is going, and so is King Archibald's captain of the guard, Captain Everhart. Horace insists on accompanying us, too.

He feels very guilty about letting you get trapped in the room that filled with water."

"But he didn't *let* me do anything!" said Annie. "He told me that going down there was a bad idea."

"He's convinced that he could have stopped you if he'd really tried, although even I know that stopping you when your mind's made up is impossible! Let me see ... oh, yes, Dog is going as well."

"That is quite a group," Annie told him.

"We don't have a lot of time to do this, and I've already explored most of the castle. The only place I haven't looked is the south tower, which was locked when I tried to go in."

"The room that filled with water was in the south tower," said Annie. "The door was open then."

"Because the witch wanted you to go in. Captain Everhart locked it after that, so I had to go to him for a key. He offered to accompany us so he could show us around. Are you sure you're up to this? You've been through a lot today."

"I'm sore—that's all," said Annie, trying not to show how much the idea of going outside frightened her. The crows had attacked her twice so far today. She didn't know how well she'd stand up to another attack. But she had to go with the group if there was even the smallest chance that Liam might run into one of the witches. "I'm not letting you do this without me."

"Then we need to head downstairs to that office

you were using. Captain Everhart brought you a surprise."

"What kind of surprise?" Annie asked.

"You'll see" was all Liam would say.

Annie was still a little unsteady on her feet, and with her hands so sore, she couldn't hold on to the railing very well. When Liam noticed this, he took hold of her elbow and helped her down the stairs. She gave him a grateful look when they reached the bottom. "Watching the princes during this competition has made me appreciate you all the more. You do things naturally that some princes wouldn't even think of doing. Can you imagine Digby helping anyone down the stairs?"

"No, I can't," said Liam. "But then I also can't imagine him finding a princess as wonderful as you and getting her to agree to marry him."

"I guess we're both lucky, then!" said Annie, and leaned in for a kiss. Her lips had scarcely touched Liam's when Dog butted the two of them with her head. She barked once, wagged her tail, and started to walk away.

"What's wrong with you?" Liam asked Dog. "Why aren't you talking?"

"Because she can't talk when she's too close to me," said Annie. "Was there something you wanted to tell us, Dog?"

Dog stopped and turned to look at them, her tongue

lolling from her mouth. "I want you to follow me. Everyone's waiting for you. We have lots to do."

"Here," said Liam. "I know how we can get there faster." Scooping Annie into his arms, he ran down the corridor, banging the door open with his shoulder. Annie was laughing as they entered the room, but her laughter died away when she saw how serious everyone looked. Horace was there with a sling on his arm and a worried expression on his face. Captain Sterling looked solemn, and standing beside him was a man Annie had seen only from a distance.

"Princess Annabelle, this is Captain Everhart," Liam said, setting her down in front of the man.

"Captain," Annie said.

"Your Highness," the captain replied. He bowed, and when Annie held out her hand, he took it and kissed the back before letting it go.

Captain Everhart was older than Captain Sterling by about twenty years, and his gray hair was turning white. Annie was conscious of his scrutiny as Liam turned her toward the table in the middle of the room.

A suit of armor, from armored foot covers to helmet, was laid out on the table's surface, and it all seemed to be her size. "What's this for?" Annie asked, glancing up at Liam.

"It's for you!" Horace announced. He had been standing in the corner, but he stepped forward now and tapped the helmet with his finger. "This'll keep the crows off you better than anything!"

"The crows won't know it's you if you go outside wearing that. It's a boy's suit of armor that Captain Everhart found," Liam said. "It's lighter than a man's armor. It may not be the best fit, but it's the closest thing to your size that the captain could find."

Annie was touched that they'd thought of the armor. Although she had tried to be brave and not show them how much the birds frightened her, she must not have been very convincing. Even thinking about the crows made her panic; facing another attack would be more than she could bear.

Liam laughed. "Think of it as an experience that you can tell our grandchildren about someday."

"I don't know if I can put it on," Annie said, holding up her bandage-swathed hands.

"We'll help you," said Liam. "All you have to do is stand there."

"But … wait! I don't … that's too … ow!"

No one listened to Annie's protests as they strapped on the leather and metal pieces of the armor. Some pieces squeezed too tight, and others cut into her a bit when she moved, but the suit of armor did fit somewhat when they had it all on her, and she could walk when she tried to, although not very fast.

"So what do you think?" Liam asked as he closed the visor on the helmet.

"I'll be fine as long as I don't take any deep breaths," Annie said, jabbing at the visor with both hands. "Would you mind putting this up again? I can't see a thing with it down."

"But do you feel safe from the crows?" asked Horace as Liam lifted the visor.

"Very safe," said Annie. "Not even the crows can get past this much protection!" She turned slowly and walked to the door, clanking loudly. "I can see that it has limitations, though. I can't run in it, I can't wear it if I want to sneak up on someone, and I don't ever want to stand outside in a thunderstorm while I'm wearing this. Come on. Dog is right. We do have lots to do."

"Captain Everhart," Liam said as they started out the door, "you think that the south tower is the only place a witch could hide in the castle?"

"I do," said the captain. "No one goes there anymore, not after Queen Marissa claimed it for her own. I know what it looked like before she came, but it's changed a lot since then. I supervised cleaning out the room she used on the top floor. It's not a room I'd enter unless I had to."

Annie froze when she reached the door leading outside and saw the crows perched on the wall. Using both hands, she lowered her visor and adjusted her head inside the helmet until she could see through the narrow slit. Her mouth was dry when she murmured, "I can do this," and she forced herself to start walking.

Finding Captain Sterling in front of her, she followed his back, taking one slow step at a time. Although she doubted that she could have made herself go outside without the helmet, wearing the visor down was unnerving. Not only was her vision limited, but her breath was loud in her ears and her scalp itched as she began to perspire.

Although Annie could hear the crows caw occasionally, she couldn't see much of anything. She thought about turning to look around, but she wasn't sure she'd find the captain again, and she liked being able to follow his back. At one point, the crows' raucous voices grew louder, and she could see Captain Sterling waving his sword. She was sure the crows were attacking, but then the captain moved on and so did she, and in a few minutes they were waiting by the tower door as Captain Everhart unlocked it.

Once they were inside the tower and the door was closed, Annie took off the helmet. After scratching her itchy scalp, she brushed the damp hair off her forehead.

"I thought we'd start at the bottom and work our way up," said Liam. "Annie, you might want to stay here."

"Then what was the point of my coming along?" she asked. "I know that horrible room is down there, but I still think I should go."

Liam shrugged. "I'm all right with it if you are. Dog, why don't you go first?"

Annie eyed the long set of stairs and thought about removing the suit of armor, almost immediately dismissing the idea. Although the armor was awkward and uncomfortable, she felt safer with it on and didn't want to take it off. Annie couldn't help but feel that here in the tower, where the witch had tried to drown her, something else had to be lying in wait. If it was a flock of crows, what better way to face them than while encased in a metal suit?

"Better safe than sorry," she muttered, tucking the helmet under her arm. Once again Liam walked beside her as she made her way down the stairs, following the islands of light from the torches that Captain Sterling and Captain Everhart had brought.

The stairs felt longer than Annie remembered, and the walk down seemed to take forever. When she reached the bottom, she stopped to look around. The floor was still damp with small puddles, and the air was cold and smelled musty. Annie didn't go in the room where she'd been locked, but Liam and the captains did. A few minutes later, Liam was gesturing to her from what she had thought was a niche in the wall but turned out to be the beginning of a short corridor.

"This is where the witch went when she locked you in that room," said Liam. "And look here—it's the lever she must have pulled to let the water in."

Annie shuddered and made a point of *not* looking. As interesting as Liam seemed to find it, she couldn't wait to get out of there. She followed him past the other two doors in the corridor, peeking inside. One was filled with broken furniture warped from all the moisture. The other held suits of armor so rusty that pieces crumbled off when Horace touched them.

"Why would you store anything in such a wet place?" Annie asked Liam.

"Who knows?" the prince replied. "It sure didn't do this stuff any good. There's no sign of any witches down here, so let's start on the higher floors."

Annie groaned as she climbed the stairs back to the first floor. There had to be at least ten floors in the tower, and she dreaded the thought of climbing to each one.

It didn't take them long to search the first floor. Aside from the staircase leading down and another leading up, there were two empty rooms with piles of moldering litter in the corners. Dust lay thick on the floor; it was obvious that no one had been in either room in a very long time. When Dog searched a room, she left paw prints in the dust. She sneezed when she snuffled the floor and came back to Annie with her muzzle gray.

"What did you smell?" Annie asked.

"Old stuff that used to be here but isn't anymore," said Dog. "Nothing good."

The next few floors held more empty rooms, but as they climbed higher, they found evidence that birds had been making their homes there. A few black feathers made Annie think that they might be the crows, and she held the helmet closer, glad that she had it with her.

They were halfway between the seventh and eighth floors when Dog raised her head and sniffed the air. "Something smells good up here!" she said, and scurried up the steps to the eighth-floor landing.

While Horace and the captains inspected the first room, Annie and Liam followed Dog to the room beyond it. Someone had been using the fireplace to cook, and a large kettle still hung over the ashes. The acrid smell of burned wood mingled with another, sweeter scent. A pile of small, dark bricks rested in the corner past the fireplace. Curious, Annie poked one of the bricks with her toe and gasped. They weren't bricks, but pieces of fudge cut into large blocks.

"There are candy canes over here," Liam said from the other side of the room. "And this looks like taffy."

"Granny Bentbone must be here!" said Annie.

Liam nodded. "That explains why they haven't been able to locate her in Dorinocco."

"We found bedding and some clothes in the other room," Captain Sterling said from the doorway. "I recognize some of the clothes. Granny Bentbone was wearing them when we took her to the tower. The rest look like some of the clothes we left for her."

"So when we took her to the tower, all we did was

take her sightseeing and give her a new wardrobe," said Annie.

"I'll have my men clean all this out of here," Captain Everhart announced. "I'll post a guard so no one can enter the tower again."

"Let's go inspect the upper floors," said Liam. "I want to see what else we can find. Dog, leave that alone. An evil witch made that candy. You don't know what she might have put in it."

"You're right," Dog said, and swallowed a bite of fudge. "It could be disgusting and icky. Just one more piece."

"Dog!" Annie cried. "You shouldn't eat chocolate anyway!"

"I'm coming," Dog muttered, giving the candy one last look.

Annie was tired and wished she could sit down, but she didn't know how she'd get back up with the armor on if she did. Instead, she made herself start up the next flight of stairs. Even before she stepped onto the landing, Annie knew she didn't like the ninth floor. It was empty, like the others, but she got the feeling that someone had just been there and was waiting for them to leave so she could come back. The other floors had been quiet simply because there was nothing there. This floor seemed ominously quiet. Annie didn't mention this to anyone, but the others must have felt something as well. Dog whined and stayed on the stairs while the others gave the floor only a cursory glance and hurried on to the next one.

"This is where Queen Marissa had her workshop," Captain Everhart said as they neared the top floor. "My men and I cleaned out all the jars and boxes while she was in the dungeon. We burned it in a bonfire outside."

"It smelled real bad," said Dog.

"I saw things in this room that...never mind," Captain Everhart said, glancing at Annie. Taking a heavy key from his pocket, the captain opened the door and stepped inside. "There isn't much left except for that table, those shelves, and the old mirror between those two windows."

Annie shuddered as she stepped into the room. She'd thought the room below it was bad, but this was much worse. A feeling of malevolence filled the room, as if the walls and floors could absorb the emotions of the occupants. It was dark inside, despite the six small windows, and even the captains' torches couldn't dispel the gloom. The stone floor was shattered in places and stained with something dark in others. The table was badly gouged and wobbled on its legs when Horace touched it. Dog sniffed at the stains and growled, walking away stiff-legged with her ears laid flat.

"What is it, Dog?" asked Annie.

"Bad things," whined Dog.

"Can you bring more light over here?" Liam asked from where he stood by the mirror.

The two captains came forward with their torches. Shadows seemed to waver and flow across the upper walls and ceiling, shying away from the light. Annie could feel the tiny hairs on her arms rise as she walked toward the mirror. She jumped when she heard a soft sound behind her, where no one had been a moment before. Spinning around, Annie was surprised to see Cat strolling into the room.

"How did you get in?" asked Captain Everhart. "I locked the door to the tower behind us."

"I came in when you did," said Cat. "You people are so unobservant!"

"Hello, Cat!" said Annie. "I wondered if I'd get to see you."

"I've been busy," Cat replied. "The dungeons were full of mice when I moved in. It's my duty to eat as many as I can."

"Someone has been here," said Liam. "Look, there are footprints in the dust on the floor. Especially here, in front of this mirror."

"The queen talked to that mirror every day," Cat declared. "Why don't you try it? Ask it a question. It will answer with pictures."

"I love pictures!" said Dog.

"How does it work?" asked Liam.

Cat yawned and stretched one back leg, then the other. "Do what the old witch did. Say 'Mirror, mirror, on the wall,' then ask your question."

Liam studied the mirror. "Do you think we could use it to find out about Marissa and Terobella?"

"You won't know until you try," said Annie. "Wait just a minute. It might work better if I'm not near it." She walked to the opposite side of the room and turned to face Liam again. "Okay, go ahead."

"Mirror, mirror, on the wall," Liam began.

A face appeared, faint at first, but it was soon clear even from where Annie stood. It glared at Liam and said, "Why should I answer you?"

"You're supposed to know everything, right?" Annie called. "Do you know who I am, Mirror?"

The mirror's expression changed from belligerence to fear when it saw Annie. "Yes, yes, I do. You're that horrid princess who destroys magic. Nothing with magic will work when you're near."

"Then you'll understand what I mean when I say that if you don't answer every question he asks, I'm going to take you home with me and put you in my bedchamber. Next to my bed. Only a few feet away from where I sleep. You'll be close to me *all* night long."

"No!" cried the face.

"And my bedchamber isn't anything like this. It hasn't changed since I was a little girl. I have a tapestry with dancing unicorns on my wall and pillows embroidered with butterflies and flowers. My favorite color is pink, and I—"

"Stop!" cried the face.

"If you don't help us now, you'll spend the rest of your existence there. Oh, and I sing a lot in my room—happy, cheerful songs!"

"Enough!" said the mirror. "I'll do it! Ask your question!"

"Very good," said Liam. "Tell me, Mirror, who has come to see you lately?"

Three images appeared in the mirror. Annie recognized Queen Marissa right away. The second was Granny Bentbone, looking older and more stooped than ever. The third was a stranger to Annie; a younger woman with piercing eyes and a cruel sneer.

"That must be Terobella!" said Annie.

"Mirror, what else have they looked like over the last few days?" asked Liam.

"Normally, I don't answer more than one question a day," said the face. "I don't have enough energy for—"

"Just do it!" snapped Captain Everhart.

The first image vanished, and a succession of others replaced it, but the images were fainter now, each one less distinct than the one before—a guard, a chambermaid, two young men...

"Wait!" cried Annie. "I recognize those men. Didn't they come with one of the princes we met here?"

"I think you're right!" said Liam. "But which prince?"

"Ask the mirror," said Cat.

"Mirror, which prince brought those men?"

"I'll try," said the face, which was becoming blurrier

by the moment. A picture appeared, but it was so faint that all they could see was a vague shape. And then it, too, was gone, and the mirror went blank, not even reflecting the people around it.

"Well, that was interesting," said Cat.

"And quite helpful as far as it went," said Liam. "Now we just have to figure out which prince they're with."

"And hope they don't do anything nasty first!" said Annie. She gasped at a sudden brilliant idea. If it worked, they could find the queen that very afternoon! "Dog, you've smelled Queen Marissa before. Do you think you could smell her if she looked like someone else?"

"If she looked like someone else, she'd smell like someone else," said Dog. "She didn't smell like the queen when she came to the cottage in a wagon."

"Oh, right," Annie said. "She was a young woman then, dressed as a tinker's wife. So much for that brilliant idea!"

"Don't worry," Liam told her. "I'm sure you'll have another."

CHAPTER 17

ANNIE WAS LOOKING FORWARD to supper that night. She hoped that seeing the princes would trigger memories of the people who had been with them when they arrived. The bandages made cleaning herself up awkward, but she managed it after a while and was ready when Liam arrived to escort her downstairs.

"I wonder if Snow White has chosen her prince yet," said Liam as they walked through the corridor.

"I think she knows who it's going to be, but she doesn't want to tell anyone until after the competition is over. It won't be long now. The last test was today."

Annie looked up as a young woman approached. It was Cynara, the girl she had asked to help with the test of honesty.

"Your Highness," Cynara said, curtsying.

"I'm so sorry, Cynara! I forgot to send the coins to you!"

"That's all right," the girl said, her cheeks dimpling when she smiled. "I did it anyway. I asked a friend to help me, and we had great fun! I thought you would like to hear our results. All the princes gave the coin back to me except for two. Digby kept it, and my friend said that he seemed quite pleased with himself. Milo kept it, too, but he treated it more as a curiosity. He made a remark about King Archibald's likeness and tucked it in his pocket. My friend wasn't sure that Milo was even aware that I had dropped it."

"Thank you so much for doing that!" said Annie. "You were very helpful. I'm sorry—I don't have any coins with me now, but—"

"I do," said Liam, handing Cynara two pieces of gold.

"Ooh, who is that on the coin?" Cynara asked, examining it closely. "I've never seen one like this before."

"That's my father, King Montague of Dorinocco," said Liam.

"I think I'll save one of them as a keepsake," Cynara said, tucking the coins into the tiny silk bag that dangled from her wrist.

"Thank you again!" Annie said as Cynara curtsied once more.

The young woman was walking way when Annie turned to Liam and declared, "So we had our honesty test after all! I must say, the results don't really surprise me."

"Me, either," said Liam. "Although I do think we're

finding out more about the princes by comparing their own stories with what the guards say they're actually doing."

"I know!" said Annie. "I can't wait to hear the new stories tonight!"

※

Snow White and most of the princes were already at the table when Annie and Liam entered the great hall.

"Annie, how are you?" Snow White asked. "I worried about you all afternoon."

"I'm fine, thank you," Annie said, aware of the curious glances of the people seated nearby.

"Why were you worried?" Emilio asked as he took his seat.

"The crows attacked Annie today!" exclaimed Snow White. "She fought them off very bravely, but they scratched her poor arms."

"Dear girl!" said the king, who had come in without Annie's noticing. "How dreadful! I see you are wearing bandages."

"Snow White helped me," said Annie. "As did Maitland and Liam."

"Then we know what Maitland's story will be tonight," said Nasheen. "Yet another tale of how he helped Princess Annabelle."

"Actually, he helped me a great deal," said Annie.

"He bound up my wound and saw that I was tended to, then got rid of the crows that had taken over my bedchamber."

"The always honorable prince," Nasheen said, sneering at Maitland. "How can the rest of us compete?"

"By actually trying," Annie said, trying not to lose her temper. She caught herself before she could say more and sat back in her seat.

Liam, however, had a gleam in his eye when he said to Snow White, "Since we've already heard Maitland's story of compassion, I propose that we hear the rest now, before we eat."

"Excellent idea!" said the king. "I'm eager to hear their tales myself. Prince Nasheen, why don't you go first?"

Nasheen looked unhappy, but he bowed his head to the king before turning to Snow White. "I was riding my stallion this afternoon when I came upon an old woman in the road. She had lost her young charges, so I helped her find them."

"That was good of you, Nasheen," said Snow White.

"I moved a turtle that was crossing the road," said Tandry. "A cart was going to run over it, but I saved its life."

"Well done," said Snow White.

King Archibald looked amused.

"Well, I rescued a drowning child!" Milo announced. "Children in Gulleer can swim before they can walk, but this poor boy was floundering in the water while his companions stood by, unaware of his pleas for help. Hearing his cries, I ran to the pond, dove into the water, and pulled him to shore."

"Brave and compassionate!" said Snow White.

"I went to a nearby village, where I found an old woman whose roof had collapsed," said Emilio. "I spent most of the day helping her fix it."

"Really!" said his cousin. "So that's where you were! I thought you were afraid of heights!"

"I managed," Emilio said, his face turning red. "And what did you do today, Cozwald?"

"I gave a cherished book to a deserving young person who I thought would benefit from reading it," Cozwald told them.

"The gift of knowledge is a gift beyond measure," said the king. "And what about you, Prince Digby?"

Digby shrugged. "I rescued some drowning kittens from a river."

"Why were the kittens drowning?" asked Annie.

"A farmer had stuffed them in a sack and tossed them in," said Digby. "I guess he didn't want so many cats."

"And that leaves you, Andreas," said Liam. "What did you do today?"

"I took a basket of food to a sick family," he said. "They were all extremely grateful."

"Quite admirable," said the king.

"May we eat now?" asked Digby. "I'm starving!"

"Rescuing kittens will do that to you," Liam told Annie as the king gestured for the servers to bring the food.

Annie studied each of the princes as they ate supper, trying to remember whom she had seen them with throughout their stay. Unfortunately, she'd been paying more attention to the women she thought might be witches than to the young men who had arrived with the princes. Maybe Liam or one of the guards had a better memory of them.

As anxious as Annie had been for supper to start, now she couldn't wait until it was over. Snow White seemed as eager to go, and Annie was just about to suggest that they ask the king's permission to leave when a serving girl set a pie in front of her.

"I was told to tell you that this was made especially for you," said the girl.

Annie glanced at the golden-brown crust on the pie. The crust looked delicious, but there was something odd about the pie. There was a funny smell, for one thing. . . . It was musky and . . .

Annie jumped up from the table. Something under the crust had moved!

"What is it?" Liam asked, and everyone else turned to her in surprise.

The bandages made Annie's hands clumsy, but she grabbed the platter that held the remains of a roasted duck and dumped the bones on the table. Crows had begun bursting through the crust when Annie slammed the platter onto the pie, fighting furiously to hold it there.

"Help me!" Annie cried, but Liam had already lunged toward the platter to add his strength to hers.

Maitland had jumped up as well, and together he and Liam wrestled the wobbling, jerking pie plate off the table while holding the platter on top.

Annie sank back in her seat as the two young men carried the platter out of the great hall.

"Get that serving girl back here!" the king growled to a guard.

Snow White put her arm around Annie's shoulders. "How awful!" Snow White cried. "And after everything that happened today!"

"I never used to think about crows one way or another, but I can honestly say that I now truly hate them!" said Annie.

"I don't blame you one bit!" her friend exclaimed.

Only a few minutes later, the serving girl was back, looking bewildered. "Yes, Your Majesty," she said, curtsying to the king. "You wanted to see me?"

"Where did you get that pie?" demanded King Archibald.

"From the kitchen, Your Majesty. One of the kitchen helpers told me to bring it and say what I said."

"Which helper?"

The girl looked even more bewildered now. "I don't

know, Your Majesty. It was so busy in there. And everyone was rushing around...."

The king glanced at Annie. Her distress must have shown on her face because he motioned to Snow White and said, "Why don't you take Princess Annabelle out of the great hall? There's no need for her to stay. I'll have my guards look into this."

"As you wish, Father," Snow White replied. She stood and turned to the princes, who were still sitting at the table. "I'll make my announcement in the morning. We'll meet here at eight o'clock instead of in the small dining hall. I hope you all have a pleasant evening."

The two girls had just entered the corridor when they ran into Liam and Maitland. Liam started walking with Annie while Snow White stayed behind to talk to Maitland.

"Are you all right?" Liam asked Annie as he put his arm around her.

"I am," she replied, leaning into his warmth. "Thank you for rescuing me yet again. I don't know what I would have done if you and Maitland hadn't jumped up to help me."

"Poor Maitland," said Liam. "He is so smitten with Snow White that he hardly touched his food. I wonder if she knows how he feels about her."

"Oh, she *knows*."

"Do you think she's forgiven him for the remarks he made about her to his friends?"

"I'm not sure, though I do know that her decision depends on it," Annie said. "She was furious with him when it happened."

When Annie and Liam reached the small dining hall, Captain Everhart was there, as well as Captain Sterling. "I want to talk to the captains about the crow pie," Liam told Annie. "I'll be with you in a minute."

Annie didn't even want to think about the crows, so she was happy to take her seat. Snow White and her father soon arrived, stopping to speak to Liam and the two captains before coming to the table.

Snow White sat down and leaned toward Annie. "Father talked to the guards. No one knows anything about the kitchen helper. She was there, then she wasn't. Maitland did tell me that when he and Liam set the pie in the courtyard, twenty-four small crows flew out and got bigger as they flew away. Now, you can't tell me that wasn't magic, too! No one could really bake birds in a pie and have them come out alive, let alone grow as they fly!"

"I'm sure magic was involved," Annie said, her stomach churning as she remembered the crows shoving their beaks through the pie crust. "The witch must have known that the magic would come undone when the girl set the pie in front of me."

"And then the crows would get big again and force their way out of the pie!"

Annie nodded. "She's a very smart witch."

"We'll begin with the guards' reports," said the king. "Who followed Prince Nasheen today? Did he really help an old woman?"

"I followed the prince," said a guard. "He was riding through your city when he almost rode over an old woman walking down a narrow road with two small children. His horse reared and the woman screamed. The two little boys ran off. The woman became frantic when she couldn't see them, and he told her which way they'd run."

"That was it?" said Snow White. "He made it sound like so much more."

"What about Milo?" asked Liam. "Did he really rescue a drowning child?"

Another guard spoke up. "He came upon a farm pond where a man was teaching his sons to swim. The youngest was kicking and splashing more than the others. I suppose it's possible that it might have looked as if he was in trouble. Prince Milo dove into the water and dragged the boy to the edge. The child was afraid of the prince and started crying. The boy's father was angry at first, but he didn't know what to do when the prince introduced himself."

"That's some rescue," said Liam.

"But it sounds as if Milo meant well," Snow White said.

"I want to hear about Andreas and the sick family," said Annie.

"Andreas did take food to a family in the city," said the guard who had followed him. "He took a basket filled with bread, wine, and cheese from the cooks in the royal kitchen and carried it to an area where the houses were in poor repair. He asked the people on the streets if they knew of a family who was sick and was directed to one of the more dilapidated cottages. When a woman opened the door, she admitted that everyone had colds, so he handed her the basket. The woman seemed more surprised and confused than anything."

"At least he tried to be helpful," said Snow White.

"Do we really have to do this?" asked Annie. "I mean, you have to know who you're going to choose by now, Snow White."

"I do," Snow White admitted, "but it's only fair to hear the other side of each of their stories. Besides, I like to hear the truth."

"And I find it highly entertaining," said the king. "Please continue. Who saw Digby rescue the kittens?"

"I did," said a guard. "He was riding beside the river when a man carrying a squirming, mewing sack tossed it into the water. Digby dismounted and used a stick to pull the sack to the water's edge. He opened the sack and looked inside. The man came over to ask what he was doing. Digby handed the sack back to him and rode off. The man tossed the sack in the river again and left."

"So the kittens drowned?" Snow White said, looking horrified.

"Uh, after Prince Digby was out of sight, I fished the sack out again and took it with me to the next village," said the guard. "Three little girls were delighted to get the kittens."

"So you were the one who actually showed compassion!" cried Snow White.

The guard looked embarrassed when he shrugged.

Captain Sterling gestured to another guard, who said, "I followed Prince Tandry. He did move a turtle off the road, although I believe the turtle would have appreciated it more if Tandry hadn't taken it back to the side from which it'd started."

Liam snorted and shook his head.

"Prince Emilio also did what he said, to some extent," said a guard. "He rode to a nearby village, where he found an old woman lamenting that her roof was collapsing. He stayed for the entire afternoon and helped her fix it; however, he helped by making her go up the ladder onto the roof while he handed her new thatching."

"He made the old woman climb around on the roof herself!" Snow White exclaimed. "That's dreadful."

"At least he tried!" Liam said with a laugh.

"And I suppose Cozwald didn't really give a cherished book to a deserving person?" Snow White asked the guards.

"Indeed he did," a guard said. "He was reading a

book in the garden when a girl dressed in dirty furs went past. I don't think she knew he was there and seemed startled when he closed the book, stood up, and handed it to her. She stammered her thanks as she took the book and ran off as if she was afraid."

"He gave a book he'd finished reading to a girl who can't read," said Liam.

Annie smiled, but she didn't say anything. She wouldn't be at all surprised if Lilah was able to read.

"And Annie has already told us of how Maitland helped her today," said the king. "Does anyone have anything to add to that?"

Captain Sterling shook his head. "Prince Maitland did everything that the princess said. I heard him ask about her later, and he seemed quite concerned."

"Very good!" said the king. "Then I believe we've heard all the reports. Thank you, gentlemen. You are dismissed. However, I want your captains to stay. We still have much to discuss. Captain Sterling and Captain Everhart have already told me what transpired today, but Snow White hasn't heard the story. Annie, if you would?"

Annie nodded and turned to her friend. "After we left your room, the gentlemen helped me put on a suit of armor, and we went outside."

"A suit of armor! What was it like?" asked Snow White.

"Hot and uncomfortable, although I was glad I had it on when the crows spotted us. Anyway, we got to the south tower, and we searched the whole thing. We found where Granny Bentbone has been living."

"Is that the old woman you told me about, Liam?" asked the king. "The one who escaped from the tower?"

"Indeed it is, Your Majesty," Liam replied.

"Was she there?" Snow White asked.

Annie shook her head. "No, so we kept looking until we got to the top floor."

"Where Marissa had set up her workshop!" exclaimed Snow White.

"Exactly!" said Annie. "Her old mirror was still there, and Cat came by and suggested that we try asking it a question. Liam asked it who had come to see it in the last few days. The visitors were your stepmother, Marissa; Granny Bentbone; and a woman I didn't recognize. I think she must be Terobella."

"The witch who'd sent Liam's mother the message!" said Snow White.

"That's right! They looked like themselves when the mirror showed them to us, but when he asked who else they had looked like here, the mirror showed us a few people—a guard, a chambermaid, and two young men."

"We think the young men came here with one of the princes who arrived before we did," Liam told Snow White. "One had brown hair and blue eyes; the other had blond hair and hazel eyes. Do you remember any men fitting those descriptions?"

"No, sorry! I was so busy looking at my prospective

bridegrooms that I didn't notice anyone else," said Snow White.

"Does anyone remember these two young men?" Annie asked the others. When no one said that they had, Annie sighed and glanced at Liam. "Then I'm afraid that we're going to have a rough morning tomorrow."

"What Annie's trying to say is that if we don't take the witches into custody before Snow White makes her announcement, they are bound to cause problems. We'll all be together in one room, so we'll be easy targets."

"I'll post extra guards," said Captain Everhart.

"My men will also stand guard," Captain Sterling told the king.

"And I'll try to find the men in the morning," Annie said. "They may have changed their appearances again, but my touch will still show them as witches."

"I think we should all try to get some rest now," said Snow White. "Tomorrow is going to be a busy day!"

Annie, Liam, and Snow White left the room when the king started talking to the captains about where the guards would stand in the great hall. Maitland was waiting outside the room, and his eyes lit up when he saw Snow White.

"So is Maitland her choice?" Liam asked as he and Annie left Snow White and the prince alone in the corridor. "He's the best of the lot, so I hope she chooses him."

"I hope so, too," said Annie. "I think they're almost as perfect for each other as we are."

CHAPTER 18

ANNIE SLEPT POORLY that night. She lay awake until
the small hours of the morning, thinking about all the
dreadful things the witches could do. When she finally
fell asleep, she had terrifying dreams that left her staring into the darkness with her heart racing.

She couldn't go back to sleep, so she tried to make
her mind go blank. Instead she ended up thinking
about the contest and what she would have done if she
had been taking the tests. Because she knew Snow
White better than any of the princes did, the first test
would have been easy. She probably would have asked
the gardener to help her plant a garden like the one
Snow White had at the cottage, or written out some of
the funny stories Snow White had told her about living
with the dwarves and then given them to her in a book.

The test for compassion would have been easy, too,
because Annie liked helping others. She often gave

clothes or food to the less fortunate at home. Helping people who wanted to see what some aspect of their lives would be like without magic was being compassionate, too, wasn't it? Looking at compassion like that made her wonder if, instead of getting annoyed when so many people asked for her help, she should think about their plights a little more and try to be a little more patient with their demands.

As for the honesty test—it never would have occurred to her to keep the coin. But while that had seemed like a good test before, she now thought that the real test for honesty had been when the princes told the stories of what they'd done.

Annie thought that the test for bravery would have been the hardest. When she tried to think of the one thing she feared the most, she remembered what Maitland had told Liam. His worst fear was that Snow White wouldn't choose him. When Annie really thought about it, she realized that her worst fear wasn't of crows or water-filled rooms or falling carriages or dangling baskets—it was that something awful would happen to Liam. He had become the one person in her life whom she thought she couldn't do without. She was happiest when she was with him. When they were apart, she couldn't wait to see him again. Annie couldn't bear to think of a future that didn't include Liam. Anything that could jeopardize that petrified her.

Annie dozed off eventually and woke to sounds in

the corridor outside her room. First she couldn't go to sleep, then she'd overslept on a morning when she had hoped to be early! A sliver of light came under the door, but it wasn't enough for her to see to get dressed, so she got out of bed and tucked back the tapestry that covered the window just enough to let in some daylight. Washing and dressing didn't take long, and she was soon hurrying down the stairs.

Even though she fairly flew down the steps and through the corridor, Annie was the last to arrive at the royal table. Liam raised a questioning eyebrow when she took her seat, but she just shook her head and reached for a piece of toast.

"We were talking last night," Andreas was telling Snow White. "We all decided that whoever is not chosen will leave right after your announcement."

"I quite understand," Snow White told him.

"The baked eggs and cheese are really good," Liam said to Annie. "You should try some."

"I'm not very hungry," Annie replied. She was holding the piece of toast in her hand, but she had yet to take a bite. The two witches might be seated somewhere at one of these tables. If she'd been here as early as she'd planned, she might have spotted them when they took their seats, but now . . .

When Snow White finished talking to Andreas, Annie leaned closer to her and whispered, "Has anyone spotted the witches yet?"

Snow White shook her head. "No, although the guards were watching for them as everyone came into the hall. Do you think they might leave without doing something horrid?"

"I doubt it very much," said Annie. "So keep your eyes open and tell me if you see anything odd."

"You should eat something," Liam said as he heaped food onto her plate. "You want to keep your strength up."

Annie eyed the toast and took a bite. She was glad when breakfast was finally over and the plates were removed.

When Snow White stood, everyone grew silent and turned her way. "First of all," she said, "I'd like to thank all the princes who participated in my contest. The trials were not always easy, but you did your best and for that you should be proud. I understand that you want to leave if you have not been chosen. To those of you who did not win, I promise you my friendship and wish you all the best in finding your own true love. Fortunately for me, this contest has allowed me to find the man with whom I wish to spend the rest of my life. My true love and the man I want to marry is Prince Maitland of Montrose."

Hardly anyone seemed surprised. Emilio shrugged and smiled at Snow White and Maitland. "Congratulations!" he said, extending his hand to the grinning prince. His cousin Cozwald also offered his hand, as did Andreas and Milo.

Prince Nasheen, however, stood and slammed his tankard onto the table, sending cider sloshing over the rim. "I knew you were going to choose him! I don't know why I bothered to participate in a contest where the winner had been determined from the start. Goodbye. I doubt I shall ever return to your kingdom."

Annie watched openmouthed as he stormed from the hall, but she kept her eyes on the men who followed him. None of them looked like the men she'd seen in the mirror.

"I must say that I am very disappointed," said Digby. "I came a long way and faced much personal danger to try for your hand. I did extremely well in each of the trials and deserve more than this."

"I'm sorry, Digby, but I've already made my decision," Snow White replied.

"Then I'm leaving, and you don't have to worry about being my friend. I don't need another princess for a friend. I have enough of those already. 'Can't we just be friends, Digby?' they say," he declared in an artificially high voice as he stalked from the table.

"If there was a contest for worst sport, I think Digby would win," said Liam.

"I don't know," said Annie. "I think Nasheen would be a real contender. Liam, where did Tandry go? He had been sitting beside Digby before Nasheen started talking, but now I don't see him anywhere."

"What's that, you say? Is Prince Tandry gone?" asked

the king. "Guard!" he called to a man standing nearby. "Find out where Prince Tandry went."

"Did anyone see him leave?" asked Annie.

"He was there one minute and gone the next," said Snow White. "I think that's odd. You told me to tell you if I saw something odd, Annie."

"You're right, I did," Annie said. "I think I should go look for him."

The guard whom the king had sent to find Tandry came hurrying back to the table. "He's in the court-yard, Your Majesty. He's preparing to leave."

"Excuse me," Annie said, getting to her feet.

Liam set his hand on her arm to stop her. "You don't have to go. It isn't safe for you out there."

"If the witch is in the courtyard, I don't have any choice," said Annie. "This is one of those times when I may be the only one who *can* help. You have to let me go, Liam. I have to do this."

Liam studied her face for a moment, then took his hand away. "Fine, but I'm going with you," he said, and stood up beside her.

Together they made their way between the tables. As soon as they were clear of the crowd, they began to run. When they reached the courtyard, it was filled with people shouting, grooms leading horses, and car-riages rattling across the cobblestones. Crows were watching from the surrounding roofs, and a few had perched atop the carriages.

Captain Sterling caught up with Annie before she could go running after Tandry. "We just saw the two men from the mirror. They were with Tandry's group."

"Maybe they're just going to leave," Liam said, sounding hopeful.

"I doubt that very much," said Annie. "I want to be ready if they have something planned. Promise me that you'll stay back if they start tossing magic around."

"And let you face them by yourself?" said Liam. "I don't think so!"

"There she is!" Tandry shouted over the voices of the crowded courtyard. "There's Princess Annie."

Annie spotted the young man standing on a crate, looking over the heads of the crowd. He was pointing right at her and talking to someone she couldn't quite see. And then the crowd moved, clearing a space between Annie and Tandry, and Annie saw the people she had been trying to find. Granny Bentbone was standing beside the two men, but as Annie watched, the men changed, turning into Queen Marissa and the unknown woman Annie had seen in the mirror.

"Stay here, Liam!" Annie said, and began walking toward the witches.

Tandry climbed down from the crate as Annie approached. He looked much younger now, closer to twelve than sixteen. He was short and scrawny and had wide-set eyes shadowed by heavy brows. It occurred to Annie that he had kept his distance from her since the very first day and had always sat as far away as he could during meals.

"It's all her fault, isn't it, Mother?" Tandry said, talking to the woman Annie thought was Terobella. "If it wasn't for her, I'd be marrying Snow White and I'd get to live in this big castle."

"Yes, son," the woman said, her eyes narrowing as Annie walked closer. "We tried to get rid of her so she wouldn't interfere, but she was too ignorant to die."

"Terobella, is it?" said Annie. "This whole thing is about your son wanting to live in a castle?"

"No, you foolish girl," Terobella said with a sneer. "There's a lot more to it than that. It started because you had my sister Marissa's husband lock her away in a dungeon. When I learned about it, I came here to set her free. Archibald began quaking in his boots and declared that his daughter had to marry right away, so I decided that he'd given us the perfect way to make the castle our own. All I had to do was make Snow White believe that my son was her best choice. She'd marry him, and our entire family would move in. There was only one thing I had to take care of first— you, the annoying busybody who was bound to interfere. I went to Treecrest and found that your father had captured our mother and planned to execute her! Mother's cousin, Mother Hubbard, talked him out of executing her, but I couldn't leave our mother in your dungeon. I told her to call to the children, knowing that it would make your father want to move her some-where far away. What better place than the old tower?"

"You knew about the tower?" said Annie.

Terobella laughed. "Who do you think built it? I kept Rapunzel there for years, but she escaped before my son could marry her. And then you took my mother there! I had the best laugh I'd had in ages! If only you had died when I wanted you to, everything would have been perfect."

"So Tandry is your son, Marissa is your sister, and Granny Bentbone is your mother," said Annie.

Terobella shrugged. "You help your relatives, and I help mine."

"I told you that you should be afraid of her," said Granny Bentbone. "Terobella is the most powerful witch around."

"What happened to the real prince of Westerling?" asked Annie. "Did you kill him or make him up?"

"The real prince of Westerling is named Marco and is two years old!" exclaimed Marissa. "Like you, most people know nothing about the kingdom of Wester-ling. The opportunity was too perfect to pass up."

"Annie, what's going on?" Snow White called. She started toward Annie, but Maitland put his arms around her and held her back.

Terobella laughed. "Oh, look! Your little friend came to join you just in time to watch me turn her lovely castle into mud. If you had but married my son," she called to Snow White, "you could have lived here forever."

"But if I can't have the castle, nobody can, right, Mother?" asked Tandry.

"That's right, son," Terobella replied.

When Terobella raised her hand, Annie began to run, but the witch just laughed and said, "Too late, girl!" as power shimmered green around her arm. With a quick downward slash, the witch threw the spell at the ground. There was a nerve-jangling rumble and the sound of something tearing as the cobblestones split, and the ground in front of Annie cracked, forming an apparently bottomless rift that ran from the castle to the wall surrounding it. Annie stopped just before the rift, certain that it was too wide to jump across.

Terobella laughed as she raised her arm again. Another flash of green and the entire castle went from gray stone to brown mud in an instant.

"What have you done?" screamed Snow White.

"Exactly what I said I was going to do," said Terobella. "I turned your lovely castle into a mud hovel. And now for the rain."

"Please don't!" cried Snow White. "This is our home! Marissa, you used to live here. How can you let her do this?"

"Let her? I *want* her to do this!" Marissa yelled. "Terobella, make it pour!"

The rain had just begun when Terobella turned to

the people who had joined Annie at the edge of the rift. Liam was there with the king as well as many of the guards. Horace looked courageous even though his face was gray with fatigue and his arm was still in a sling.

"Now for the part we've all been waiting for—at least I have!" cried Terobella. Raising both of her arms above her head, she turned to face Annie and the crowd gathered behind her. Annie felt awful that she hadn't been able to stop the witch, but if Terobella made a mistake now...

Although others had already run from the castle grounds, Annie stood with her head high, watching Terobella's every move.

"You think I'm going to try a spell on you, don't you?" shouted the witch. "But I've had too many people warn me about you, girl." Bringing one of her arms down abruptly, she pointed her finger at Horace. A burst of green light shot at the old man, hitting his chest. Four people behind him were hit as well, and as the light began to grow, they began to shrink. In moments, they had all turned into earthworms writhing on the ground.

"That's enough!" cried Annie. "Your problem is with me, not them. What is wrong with you? You're acting like a petulant child!"

"Ah, a new approach. First your friend pleads; now you think that insulting me will make me stop."

"I don't think anything will make you stop!" Annie shouted. "I think you're an evil-spirited woman who likes the reaction she gets when she does something truly horrible. I think you like seeing the expressions on people's faces when you perform your nasty magic!"

"Perform?" Terobella said, her eyes gleaming.

"Yes, perform, like a traveling juggler out to make a few coins by amazing the crowds, or, in your case, horrifying them. I bet you do magic only when you have an audience to watch you! And I bet that your magic is the only excitement in your life! If you're not doing magic, you're sitting at home in your swamp, feeding maggots to your pet crows and watching the swamp fleas bite your son!"

"How did you—" began Tandry.

Annie could see that the witch was getting mad. Her face was turning red, and two veins stood out in her forehead. "That's why you're here, isn't it?" Annie shouted. "It's not because you love your family, but because you were bored and this was a chance to stir things up, to have a little fun in your miserable, boring life! Your sister and your mother don't mean any more to you than your son does!"

"Quiet, you piece of pestilence!" Terobella screamed.

"Why should I?" Annie shouted back. "You're afraid of me. What are you going to do—turn me into a worm, too?"

"I should!" Terobella shrieked. "Or a slug! No, no, I

have it! I'll turn you into the slime that the slugs leave behind. And when I'm done, the rain will wash you away and it will be as if you never existed!"

"Terobella, no!" shouted Marissa, but her sister was already raising her arm and pointing her finger at Annie.

Once again, a burst of green light shot from the witch's hand, but when it hit Annie, there was a loud fizzing sound, and the light rebounded, flying back to engulf Terobella. There was a flash and a bang, and she was nothing but a slime trail shining on the mud. At the same instant, Horace and the others turned back into men, the rift closed with a wet slapping sound, and the mud buildings turned back into stone. The rain began to lessen until it was gone, leaving everyone soggy but grinning.

"You did it!" Liam cried, running across the courtyard to pick Annie up and squeeze her tight.

"I remembered how Nasheen had made me mad at supper one night, and I thought that if I could only make Terobella lose her temper, she might forget that she shouldn't cast a spell at me. Then Marissa shouted and . . . where are Marissa and Granny Bentbone, by the way?"

Liam raised his head to look and smiled at what he saw. "It seems they're in Captain Everhart's custody and headed toward the dungeon."

Annie turned in Liam's arms. "What's Tandry doing?"

"It looks as if he's trying to find something in the mud. His mother has probably already washed away, though. I think we've seen the last of her."

"And the crows?" Annie asked, looking toward the top of the curtain wall.

"Gone, every last one of them, apparently," said Liam.

"Thank goodness!" Annie exclaimed. "If I never see another crow, I'll already have seen too many!"

※

After being a worm, Horace was too shaken to go anywhere that day, so Annie and Liam postponed their trip back to Treecrest until the following morning. Once again, Snow White insisted that they take gifts with them, so while Liam supervised their packing, Annie went to see Lilah. A cook's helper directed Annie to the garden, where she found Lilah reading a book.

"If you still don't want me to introduce you to Snow White, I think you should come with us," Annie told her. "Unless you have some reason to want to stay in Helmswood."

"I'm in Helmswood only because I walked this far and wanted to rest for a time. Nothing's keeping me here," said Lilah.

"Treecrest is farther from the ocean and anyone who might know your father. I can help you start a new life, and I know a lot of eligible princes if you're interested."

"Will that nice prince who gave me this book be in Treecrest?" Lilah asked, looking hopeful.

"His name is Prince Cozwald, and he'll be traveling with us for most of the way. All the princes who came with us decided to wait for us to leave. They're getting ready to go right now."

"Are you sure I wouldn't be imposing?" Lilah asked.

"I'm positive!" said Annie. "How long will it take to get your possessions together?"

"This is all I have," said Lilah.

"Then come with me! We'll be leaving as soon as we say good-bye to everyone."

When Annie and Lilah reached the courtyard, Liam was ready to go. Annie's horse was saddled, and the princes were already starting across the drawbridge.

"Who is that?" Liam asked as Lilah climbed into the back of the cart that Horace and another guard were driving.

"A friend," said Annie. "I'll tell you all about her later."

"I found her!" Dog barked when she saw Annie. The animal started running, and Annie braced herself for an enthusiastic greeting.

"Annie, there you are!" called Snow White, hurrying across the courtyard. She sidestepped Dog, who was wagging her tail and wiggling all over as she licked Annie. "We wanted to say good-bye. Thank you so much for all you've done. Without your help, I never would have known what to do about the princes or realized the truth about Maitland. And Terobella... I hate to think of what she would have done!"

"That's enough, Dog! I love you, too," Annie said, calming the animal by scratching her behind the ears. She glanced up at Snow White and smiled. "You're most welcome, Snow White. I think we all learned a lot over the past few days."

"Indeed we have," King Archibald said, giving his daughter an affectionate look. "I've already sent the royal physician packing. He was here because Marissa had brought him to the castle. I didn't know how bad he was until Snow White pointed it out. Now that we have an excellent herbalist in our midst, we don't need someone like him. You should see the plans for an herb garden that my daughter has drawn up."

"I can't wait to see your garden when it's finished," said Annie.

"You'll be back long before then!" Snow White declared. "Maitland and I want you and Liam to come to the wedding."

"Oh, I'm sure we'll be here for that!" Annie glanced at Liam, who was laughing at something Maitland had said. Liam turned just then and caught her eye. Annie nodded, then gave her friend a hug. "It's time for us to go. Good-bye, Your Majesty. Thank you for your gracious hospitality."

"It was my pleasure," said the king. "You are most welcome here anytime. You saved Snow White's life and brought her back to me, then you helped her find her true love and saved us all from a dreadful fate. My daughter couldn't have a better friend than you. Thank you for everything."

Annie was surprised when the king gave her a hug, and even more when Maitland kissed her on the cheek as he helped her onto her horse.

"We're almost relatives now, you know," Maitland told her as he checked her horse's girth. "Your sister *is* married to my brother. If Nasheen had known that, he would have suspected a conspiracy from the start."

"And he would have been wrong," said Annie. "You had to show Snow White what you were really like, and she had to get past her anger over what you told your friends and forgive you. I'm thrilled that it all worked out so well."

"Annie," Liam said, "I think the princes will be wondering what happened to us if we don't go now."

"You're right," Annie told him. "Good-bye, everyone! We'll see you soon!"

Dog followed them, barking "Good-bye!" all the way to the drawbridge.

Annie had turned back to wave to her friends one last time when she noticed that the castle looked a little odd. It took her a minute to realize why it didn't look the way it usually did. The edges of the stone weren't quite as straight as they had been before, and the corners were all a little rounded.

"Maitland and I saw it, too," Liam said when he followed her gaze. "The stones look like they did when the rain started dissolving the mud."

"It's good that they didn't stay mud any longer," said Annie. "If they had, the rain would have washed more away, and the castle would have looked very strange. You know, people often question stories of magic, but no one will ever doubt what happened here once they see the castle. So tell me, what was in the cart that Horace was driving?"

"Our gifts from Snow White! She gave you the suit of armor that you wore into the south tower."

"Really?" said Annie. "I doubt I'll ever wear it again."

"She also gave you her stepmother's magic mirror."

"Why? That thing must have been dreadful to carry down all those stairs."

"My guess is that she gave it to you because she didn't want it in her castle, although she said it was because Captain Everhart told her that it didn't answer my last question, so it has to go sit beside your bed."

"Oh my! I never really meant that!" said Annie. "It was just a threat to make it answer you."

"Well, now you're stuck with it, although I'm not so sure I want it in your bedchamber. I don't like the idea of that creature...face...whatever it is, being that close to you."

"Liam, are you jealous?"

"All the time! I'm just very good at hiding it. And that brings me to something else I wanted to discuss with you. Snow White and Maitland are going to start planning their wedding. I think we should do the same."

"Plan their wedding?" Annie said with a twinkle in her eye.

Liam laughed and shook his head. "No! Plan ours. I don't want a long engagement. Let's get married soon!"

"My parents just paid for one wedding. I'm not sure they'll be ready for another yet."

"Then we'll run off and get married in a country chapel."

"If I tell my mother that you said that, she'll have a huge wedding planned for us within a day!"

"In that case, I'll tell her myself! I love you, Annie," Liam said, bringing his horse next to hers.

She was about to reply, but the kiss he gave her took all her attention for a very long time.